through the SN❄W

kennie mae evvie

Paperback ISBN: 979-8-9890589-5-2
eBook ISBN: 979-8-9890589-6-9

Library of Congress Control Number: 2025921538

Published in 2026 by Half Note Publishing.

Printed in the United States of America.

Trigger warning: drug use and alcohol consumption

more by kennie mae

<u>Dreams in New York Series</u>

Find a Penny

Make a Wish

Through the Snow

for Scott -
thanks for choosing me

prologue
lucy

I think I'm stuck.

You know that feeling when you try to put on pants with holes in the knees and your big toe sticks on the hole and rips it even further as you stumble onto the floor, somehow unable to get your toe anywhere other than that darn ripped hole?

That's how life feels sometimes.

I know it's not a permanent feeling. I'm going to get my jeans on right, it's just a matter of how I'm going to get out of the situation I'm in. Out of the metaphorical pant leg, if you will. Or *into* it, I suppose.

My life is good. Really good, actually.

I have a good apartment with my best friend, I have an incredible relationship with my family. I have a stable job in the family business. I have it made.

But sometimes, it still feels like something's missing.

My mother will tell you it's a man that's missing. She's a hopeless romantic who married the boy next door when she was nineteen.

My cousin, Jenny, will tell you it's because I'm not at my dream job. Though, I'd argue I'm pretty close to it.

My brothers will tell you it's because I'm too much of a people pleaser, but what do they know.

If you ask me, I think we're supposed to feel stuck sometimes. Especially at twenty-five. We're not supposed to have it all figured out, all the time. The feeling that we're suffocating in our jeans is just nature's way of telling us we need more. Reminding us that there's so much out there we've yet to discover. Pushing us toward the things that make us feel uncomfortable, because you're never comfortable trying to wiggle into a pair of ripped jeans, but you know the second that zipper zips, you're going to look amazing.

But enough with the jeans metaphor.

Maybe feeling stuck isn't such a bad thing.

Maybe it's all we need to realize that life is so much bigger than us, we just have to be willing to find it.

chapter one
wyatt

"You look like crap," I say as I walk into the office and drop myself into the leather chair across from Walker.

He doesn't look up from the stack of papers on the desk as he replies, "You sure you're not looking in a mirror?"

I laugh once, but he doesn't. "What's wrong, man?"

He runs a hand down his face, clearly exhausted. "I just didn't get a lot of sleep last night. Lincoln's being a bit of a pill about his bedtime these days."

"I'll never understand why kids don't want to go to bed. Bedtime is my favorite time of day." I prop my feet on the edge of my desk, leaning back on two legs of the chair. Technically, it's our desk since there's only one office and we're co-owners, but I use it much more than he does, so in my head it's always just been mine.

He rolls his eyes as he shoves my feet off and they land with a loud thud. "I'm pretty sure you gave mom the hardest time about your bedtime when you were five."

"It wasn't fair. You and Winnie always got to stay up late."

"I was thirteen when you were five, of course I stayed up later. What's Lincoln's excuse?" he mumbles as he shuffles papers on his desk.

"He's five, that's his excuse."

"He threw the worst tantrum of his life last night. He finally fell asleep on the living room floor well past midnight. I'm pretty sure he just exhausted himself."

"Why are you here, then? It's Sunday."

When Walker opened his restaurant in Poughkeepsie he insisted on closing on Sundays. Said if he couldn't make enough money to survive the other six days a week, he shouldn't be in business with himself. He wanted a day for family time. I couldn't blame him. If I was living in the same house with Ellie and Lincoln, I'd never want to leave either.

The thought leaves a bad taste in my mouth. One that tastes a lot like jealously and I swallow hard. It's not Walker's fault he has everything I don't.

"I wanted to finalize some of the numbers," he mumbles absentmindedly. His eyebrows bunch at whatever he's seeing on the paper he dug up from the bottom of the stack.

"I gave you the numbers, like, two weeks ago. We're fine. The loan already went through."

"I know, I just wanted to double check."

"What, you don't trust me?"

A lot has changed over the years and we're closer than ever, but some things will always be off. This being one of them.

Walker offered me a job at the restaurant four years ago, before it even opened, with the caveat that I had to go back to school for accounting and get my CPA license. He even offered to help pay for school. Told me I would have a temporary position until I finished and once that was done, I'd be named the CFO and part owner.

We both kept up our bargains and when *Abe's Place* opened a little over two years ago, I helped Walker in all the ways I could. When I graduated with my MBA six months ago, he made me partner.

But no matter how much we mend the past, it's still there and I often find Walker staying late to double check my work before he goes home. I don't say anything, knowing full well I deserve the distrust no matter how much I try to overcome the choices I've made and the ripple effect they've had on everyone in my life. People can change all they want, but that doesn't erase who they were.

He finally looks up at me. "Of course, I trust you, Wyatt, but this is a big deal. If we're going to expand we need to be positive we can close for a couple months."

I raise my eyebrows. "Months? I thought this was, like, a six-week thing."

He shrugs. "I'm not sure how long the renovations will take. Tearing down an entire wall is kind of a big deal. I'm hoping we can still stay open through some of it and just close off half the dining room, but I have no idea."

"Have you found a contractor yet?"

"Yes, actually. Dannie suggested it. The owner used to work for her dad."

He moves the mess on his desk around. I'm not sure if he's actually looking for something or just needs something to do with his hands. Probably both. Walker doesn't do well with lack of sleep. "I know it's here somewhere," he mumbles.

"You must really be tired, man. I've never seen you so disorganized."

He ignores me as he finds a business card and hands it to me. "I was going to call on Friday, but I forgot."

The business card is simple. It's white with a blue snowflake in the background and the words *Snow Better Builders - General Contracting* scrawled across the center.

I raise an eyebrow. "*Snow Better Builders*? Really?"

"It's their last name."

I glance back down at the card and see *The Snow Family* at the bottom with a phone number.

"I'm really hoping you can take the reins on this one," Walker implores. "With Jason gone, I'm going to be spending even more time in the kitchen until I can find a replacement."

I scoff. "Jason was terrible and didn't do anything. Will it even be much different with him gone?"

He sighs. "You make a valid point."

"You really need to learn to fire these people," I shake my head.

Walker's notorious for being too lenient with his employees. It's worked throughout the years for the few who value a boss that doesn't micro-manage and understands people have personal lives. But there's always one who takes advantage, and Walker is much too nice to ever utter the words, 'you're fired.'

"I'll call the contractor and see when he can meet. Do you want it to be a time you can join?"

"Honestly, I'm not that worried about it. You know what we want to do. We just need some ideas drawn up and a plan. You can take care of it, right?"

"Can do, boss."

He gives me an impatient look. "You know I hate when you call me that."

I grin. "That's why I do it, brother."

"I also hate that."

"Yeah, well," I give him a playful punch on the arm, "You used to hate *me* and now look at us, joking around."

He rolls his eyes. "We need to get on some interviews. I'm already short-staffed, but we really need to get people in before the renovations are done."

"Already on it, man. Darrin interviewed a couple prep cooks this week. He gave me a list yesterday. You can look through it tomorrow and schedule second interviews if you want, but I trust Darrin. He's the best sou chef in town."

"I saw the resumes when I got in, but they're all asking for way more than we can pay. I think we should –"

"Don't think about that right now, Walker. I got it. I'll call the contractor and figure out all the numbers. Just go to the game."

"Right, the game, yes. Are you coming?"

I nod. "Planning on it."

He checks his watch and groans. "Ugh, I'm gonna be late. And to the first game of the season. Dannie's gonna kill me."

He gathers everything off his desk in a rush, folding and bunching pages as quickly as possible into his backpack.

"Can I watch?"

"I seriously hate you," he shouts over his shoulder as he bolts out the back door.

Walker and I have had our ups and downs over the years, but the last four years have been great. He's honestly the best brother a guy could ask for. I'd never admit that to him, but he knows it anyway. He's done more for me than I ever deserved. So has Ellie. Or as she more commonly goes by these days, Dannie.

When I knew Dannielle Brookes, she was just a bright-eyed freshman at NYU. Sometimes it feels like two different people. The Ellie I used to know and the Dannie I know today. But I think she likes it that way, separating the two lives. When I came back into her life, I wondered if she'd ask me to call her Dannie, but she hasn't said a word. She'll always be Ellie to me.

I shut off all the lights and make sure the doors are locked before climbing into my car.

Lincoln's baseball hat is in the passenger seat from the day before when I took him for ice cream. I smile at the memory of his messy chocolate face grinning at me.

Ellie was so angry when we drove up.

"He's five years old, Wyatt. He can't sit in the front seat."

"It's less than a mile, Ellie, and he was having a good time."

Her hands rested on her hips impatiently. "You need to learn how to tell him no."

"That's what his parents are for," I argued.

She opened her mouth as if to argue that I, too, was a parent, but we both know I'm not. Not really.

I pull out of the parking lot as I shove the memory from my brain. I hit the gas a bit too aggressively, trying my best to forget about the past and what could've been.

chapter two
lucy

"Life's too short to waste it on men."

I look at my cousin, Jenny, and try to hide my laugh behind my sparkling water.

"I'm just saying, dear, you're not getting any younger," my great-aunt Janice says for what must be the eighth time in the last fifteen minutes. "Your eggs will dry up. You have to start taking things seriously."

Jenny scoffs. "Seriously? You realize the pool of men has dwindled to nothing but homewreckers and superhero cosplayers, right?"

"Cosplayers?" Janice mouths with a look of concern on her face. "I'm not sure I know what that means. Regardless, you won't find what you're not looking for."

"Exactly," Jenny agrees. "That's why I'm not looking. Who needs a boyfriend when you have a fully stocked bookshelf?"

I have to stifle my laughter as I stand there quietly listening to them go back and forth for another ten minutes.

My whole family has gathered at my parents' house for a party. To celebrate what, I'm not sure. I think one of my nephews won a basketball game or something last night. We don't usually get together on Sundays, but the Snows will find any reason to throw a party. Birthdays, Christmas, Easter, St. Patrick's Day, heck, even Flag Day parties are a hoot with my family. Last year my dad ordered an ice sculpture of Sylvester Stallone for International Boxing Day. Like I said, we love a good party.

"What about you, Lucy Rae?" Janice finally turns her attention to me. "How are things?"

"Good," I force a smile, keeping my answer short. With Aunt Janice, less is always more. She'll take the smallest thing you say and run with it in ten different directions. You tell her about the cute flight attendant who told you your eyes looked like the ocean and the next thing you know your parents are calling in a panic, thinking you're moving to Argentina with the flight attendant you met on your weekend trip to Cancun. Jenny's still laughing about that one.

"Still working for your dad?" she asks.

I nod.

"It's so great that you can join the family business. A girl like you needs to stay close," she says with a patronizing pat on my arm.

I do my best to ignore the "girl like you" comment and smile. Jenny nudges my shoulder with a faint scoff.

"Yeah, it's great," I lie through my teeth.

My dad runs his own contracting firm, *Snow Better Builders* and I've been his assistant since I was sixteen. Though, assistant isn't large enough a word to truly encapsulate all I do these days.

In the last few years, I've essentially become the head project manager without any of the benefits or title. I schedule everything, communicate with all vendors and clients. I've written up every single contract in the last twelve months and processed all the payroll while my brother has been out on paternity leave. I'm never afraid to get my hands dirty and pull out my steel-toed boots whenever someone on the crew calls in sick or we're just running behind. The list goes on and I know everyone thinks they do the most at their job, but I'm an administrative assistant whose job description consists of only one sentence. Literally. All it says is, 'Miscellaneous filing and data entry.' My dad had the job description written when I was fifteen just for something in the books when I started. Pretty sure operating an excavator and installing trusses doesn't fall under 'miscellaneous filing,' but call me crazy.

Honestly, I'm not entirely sure why my father is so against the idea of me being a project manager. I could say it's because I'm his only daughter or possibly that I'm the baby of the family. Or maybe it's because he has this archaic idea that I belong in the kitchen with a baby on my hip. I honestly don't know. I've brought the idea up a time or two in the last a couple months, but he always says the same thing. "Not right now, Lucy Rae," which sets my teeth on edge. No matter how many ways I ask the same question, I manage to hear the same five words back. It's infuriating.

I love my father, please don't get me wrong. My parents are two of the best people I know and have loved me, supported me, held me when I cried and spoiled me rotten my entire life. They've spent their whole lives dedicated to their family since they got married at nineteen and had a baby exactly nine months later (we're still questioning that timeline). They've always been happy, through the good and the bad, and my brothers all have incredible families and successful careers. They've created a beautiful life and they're the two greatest people I know.

They've continued to support my goals and aspirations throughout my life. They even helped pay for my college education which was in construction management with a minor in architecture. They've always known what I wanted out of my life and career, but when it comes to actually living it, I get "not right now." It's like they've picked out this pattern for my life and have yet to share it with me.

"Oh, thank the angels she's gone," Jenny sighs beside me, slumping against the wall as Janice heads towards the kitchen.

"Is it just me or is she getting worse?" I question, taking a sip of my water.

"She's getting *old*." Jenny rolls her eyes and tosses back the rest of her drink with a noisy gulp.

"How many champagnes have you had today?"

"Not nearly enough. You?"

"Just the sparkling water for me." I hold up my alcohol-free flute glass.

"I'll never understand how you suffer through these things without the numbing delight of alcohol."

Me either, I think. I've never been a big drinker. On my twenty-first birthday, my brothers took me to a bar and I had one beer and threw up approximately two minutes after I drank the second gulp. That was the last of my drinking days. Jenny got me a glass of wine once, which wasn't terrible, but I had a horrible headache for three days. I learned quickly I was the biggest lightweight known to man and lost all interest in it after that.

"What's up with you tonight? You're quiet."

I shrug. "Just tired, I guess. Work's been busy."

"Is your dad still being a snub and ignoring the fact that you do everything?"

Jenny's never been one for subtlety.

"I mean...he's not *not* ignoring it."

She shakes her head and stands straight. "Look, I love Uncle Nick like he's my own father, but we both know he still thinks you're fifteen. You have to fight for yourself, Luce.

You're not going to get anywhere in life by living in your dad's shadow."

Jenny's only six days older than me. More like a sister than a cousin. Something I'm forever grateful for considering I'm eleven years younger than my closest sibling. My parents thought they were done having kids when they had my brother, Landon. My mom was almost thirty and had three beautiful children. They decided they were done. Until a high school reunion ten years later where they thought it would be fun to revisit the basement closet they used to hide from my grandparents in. Trust me, no one should have to know where or when they were conceived. But, needless to say, I came along as a beautiful surprise just nine months later.

Jenny was planned and is an only child. Her family lived down the street my whole life and we bonded quickly. Her dad, Matt, is my dad's youngest brother. They started *Snow Better Builders* together when I was nine. They'd been talking about opening their own business for years, but it wasn't until my dad lost his job that they finally decided to go for it. It took a few years to get things off the ground, but they did it. And *Snow Better Builders* has been the largest construction company in Poughkeepsie ever since.

Jenny and I started working for our dads in high school. Jenny moved on; I didn't. Jenny had a passion for human resources. I know, who in the world has a *passion* for HR? But she loves it. She found a job right out of college for the city and has been there ever since.

I went to college for construction management because I thought it would show my dad how serious I was about joining the family business. I'd been talking about it since I could talk and architecture shouldn't have been a surprise. I was drawing whole towns when I was in kindergarten. I think they still have my picture hanging in the office at my elementary school. I thought I'd come back from NYU with an office and a pay raise, but luck was not on my side.

"Give 'em hell. Use your claws," she says with a demonstration of her nails in my face.

I hold up my perfectly manicured nails that couldn't possibly get shorter. "You mean these claws?"

She drops her hands at her side with a sigh. "You know what I mean. I get that it's your dad, but you know he's taking advantage of you."

"He's not taking advantage of me," I defend. "He just...relies on me."

She rolls her eyes. "Same thing."

"Not all of us can get our dream job right out of college."

She smirks. "Well, not everyone can be this powerful. There isn't enough room in the world." She nods toward my brother across the room. "Have you talked to Landon about it?"

I shake my head. "Landon's busy enough with the new baby, I don't want to bother him."

She gives me a side-eye look.

"What?" I ask.

"You know what. Stop acting like everyone's life is more important than yours. You have stuff you want to accomplish, too. And it's just as important as your brothers."

This is why Jenny is my best friend.

I nudge her shoulder with mine. "You know I love you, right?"

"Yeah, yeah, buy me something pretty," she grumbles, looking over the top of my head. "Crap, she's coming back. Let's blow this popsicle stand before I have to tell her I've chosen to become a nun for the sole purpose of avoiding the opposite sex."

I laugh as she pulls my hand and drags me out the front door.

"The enchilada is so good, but I won't be able to walk for two days after eating it," Jenny says as she contemplates the menu of our favorite taco truck on Main.

"I'll stick with my grilled chicken taco, Daniel."

"Just cilantro, right?" The owner asks.

"You got it." I turn toward Jenny. "We come here too often. Not only do I know the owners name, but he knows my order."

"Well, if you mixed it up every once and a while," she argues before ordering the enchiladas.

"One or two?" Daniel asks.

"You think one enchilada will fill me? Ha! Give me three."

He chuckles as he turns back to the stove.

"So, I have an idea," Jenny starts.

"Oh goodness, do I even want to know?"

"Oh, you want to know. But you'll have to remain in suspense because if I don't find a bathroom I'm going to have to pee on the begonias."

"You'll probably have to go to the park bathrooms across the street."

"What is it with businesses not letting you use their bathrooms? Like I'm not allowed to pee until I buy a blender," she groans before hurrying across the street.

I stand on the corner, waiting for our name to be called, aimlessly scrolling through my phone when someone body slams into me.

My phone flies out of my hand and I almost stumble off the curb, but a hand is there to pull me back.

"So sorry about that," a male voice says. "I didn't see you there."

"You didn't see me standing on the curb?" I ask looking up at a man who's probably in his late thirties. His hair looks too slick and he's wearing a button up, tucked into what I would assume are very expensive jeans.

"Well, I must admit I did see you. That was the problem." He chuckles lightly, his shoulder moving in rhythm with his fake laugh. His hand still around my arm. "I've just never seen anything so beautiful, I got distracted."

His smile is cocky and the wink that follows the ridiculous pickup line gives me the ick. Does this kind of stuff usually work for him?

His hand is still holding my arm, making it difficult for me to move, leaving a nasty feeling in my stomach. Where is Jenny?

I twist my arm as subtly as I can out of his grip. "Thanks for the save. Enjoy your dinner."

"It would be more enjoyable if you joined me." He's smiling like he's already received my acceptance, moving his body just enough that's it's not really noticeable to anyone walking past, but enough to make it hard for me to move.

"I'm with a friend."

He looks around me, but Jenny is still nowhere to be seen. "I don't see any friends."

"Well, I am, and she'll be back any minute now. Have a nice day." I try to take a step around him, but he moves in front of me once again. Does this guy have no shame?

"Come on, it's just sharing a table. It's the friendly thing to do."

I try to muster as much sternness into my voice as I can when I say, "No. Now please leave me alone."

I wait for him to get irritated and leave, but he moves closer still.

He licks his lips, that stupid smile still on his face and I'm about ready to sucker punch him, when I feel someone's arm around my shoulders.

Thank you, Jenny!

I look over to give her my look of silent appreciation, but it's not Jenny that's standing next to me.

I move my gaze from the muscular chest that is in my eyesight to the dark-haired, stranger standing so close I can't hardly see anything else. His voice is deep and rough when he says, "She asked you to leave. I suggest you listen."

The long-nosed flirt looks my savior up and down as if sizing him up. He must decide he doesn't stand a chance, because he scoffs once, puffing out his chest before turning away and walking across the street. Good choice. The man next to me has to be at least six-foot-three, towering over everyone. I can't hardly see his face from where I'm standing.

The arm around my shoulder slowly slides away and I look up to the kind stranger, a thank you on my lips, but I stop short when my eyes catch his.

His hair is dark, almost black. His eyes even darker. Soft locks of hair rest delicately in every which way. It's long enough I could run my hands through it, but short enough to still be professional. Why I'm thinking about running my hands through a stranger's hair is beyond me.

His five o'clock shadow highlights his cheekbones in the best way and for a split second I wonder if greek gods are real. I don't know how long I stare at him, mouth agape, but it's much longer than is socially acceptable. Finally, I stammer, "Thanks for that."

"No problem," he replies, his voice just as deep as before, but much soft now that it's aimed at me. "You looked uncomfortable."

"I was. He would not take no for an answer."

"Are you okay?" he asks, his eyebrows coming together.

I wave him off. "Oh, yeah, I've dealt with worse."

He scowls at that as if the idea of me dealing with entitled, egotistical men upsets him.

"Thank you though, for stepping in. If I'd waited for my friend, she would've kicked him in the groin."

"That wouldn't have been so bad." His smile is barely there, but I see it and I don't want to see anything else ever again.

"You don't know Jenny's strength. She's like a marine. One knee to the groin and he'd be hospitalized. Might even have to amputate," I pretend to think about it. "Actually, you're right, that might not have been so bad."

His smiles widens to a full grin and he shoves his hands in his pockets.

"So, you aren't actually here alone? I figured that was just what you said to make him go away."

"No, my friend is with me, she's just in the bathroom."

As if she heard me talking about her, she suddenly appears beside me. "Sorry, the line was super long. Don't people have lives? Why is everywhere out here tonight?"

It takes her a second to notice the tall man standing in front of me, but when she does her eyes bug out of her head.

"Well, hello, there," she says in a sultry voice and I roll my eyes.

He gives her a simple, singular nod before turning back to me. "Well, I'm glad you're okay. You two have a good night."

"Thank you," I reply, but I'm not sure he heard me, his long stride taking him out of earshot quickly. He walks with his hands in his pockets and doesn't turn back. I stand there watching him until he turns the corner, out of sight.

"Well, well, well," Jenny says. "I could watch him walk away from me all day." She turns back to me. "Do you know him?"

I shake my head. "No. He was just helping me with this idiot that was hitting on me and wouldn't take no for an answer."

"What do you mean helping you?"

"He just came over and told the guy to leave me alone."

"You mean, that tall drink of water came over to you, a complete stranger, and saved you from another man?"

I nod.

"And you let him walk away?"

"I said thank you," I defend, not sure why she's looking at me like I have seven heads.

"You should've said, marry me! Take me home! Take me where you want because you're the sexiest man alive."

I laugh, rolling my eyes. "You are so ridiculous."

"Lucy, that man just took time out of his evening to save a damsel in distress and you just *let him walk away?*"

"Jenny, he was just being nice," I respond as Daniel calls my name. I grab our food while Jenny stands there staring.

"I can't believe you sometimes. No man is that nice."

"Maybe you haven't been hanging around the right kind of men.

"Well, obviously. If I was hanging out with the right kind of men, I wouldn't be here with you."

I laugh once as we find an empty bench and can't help but glance at the corner where my rescuer disappeared hoping to find him standing there.

But when I sneak a glance, it's just an empty corner.

chapter three
wyatt

"Lincoln, if I have to tell you one more time not to run in this house," Ellie yells. She sounds like a broken record. The kid couldn't stop running if his legs disappeared. I swear he would still find a way somehow, someway.

He doesn't stop the running as he throws his arms in the air, making little fists. "But I have to run, Mommy. I *have* to."

"Then run outside."

"But I want to run inside."

"You know the rules, Lincoln."

He's still in his soccer jersey from the game because he refuses to take it off. I'm pretty sure he sleeps in it.

His little face turns into a pinched pout, and he storms outside, nose in the air.

"He spends an hour running around a soccer field and it still doesn't tire him out," Ellie says plopping on the couch next to me. "Where does the energy come from and how do I get it?"

"You don't. It just dwindles more and more as you get old."

She scowls at me. "Old is a bad word."

I laugh as she chucks a sofa pillow at me. "He's getting better."

The scowl immediately disappears and is replaced by one of the most genuine smiles I've ever gotten from her. "He's amazing. The coach thinks we can put him in club next year."

"That's incredible."

"It *is* incredible, thank you! Tell Walker that."

"What?"

She sighs as she rests her elbow on the back of the couch and tucks her legs beneath her. It's times like this when she reminds me of the Ellie I used to know, relaxed and carefree. "Walker is under the impression that putting him in club will ruin the fun. Right now he just plays, there aren't winners or losers. I mean, they all got ribbons tonight. Walker thinks the competition of club might take away the joy of the game."

I shrug. "That makes sense, I guess."

"Does it?" she asks and I nod. "Did you ever feel that way about football?"

Her question catches me off guard. We don't talk about the past often. I'm not sure if it's because she's afraid of what happens if we do or she simply doesn't want to remember it, but I never bring it up. I made my choices and do my best to live with them.

I think for a moment before I answer. "A little, yeah. The pressure became too much. It turned into satisfying everyone else and the joy kind of...got lost, I guess."

She looks at me intently but says nothing.

"I mean," I continue shifting in my seat. "Lincoln's five. I didn't experience that until college. Different things. I loved football when I was a kid. I'm sure he'd be fine."

She opens her mouth like she wants to say something, but I cut her off.

"How's your friend? Pam was it?" I run my hands on my jeans awkwardly.

"Penny? She's good. She's due any day now. I keep waiting for a call."

Her friend, Penny, I guess, came to Lincoln's fifth birthday party a couple months ago with her husband. Her and Ellie met at Walker's restaurant in the city years ago. I think Penny moved away before Walker and Ellie ever got married, but I'm not positive of the timeline. I wasn't around back then.

"You guys going to go out and visit them? It's been a while, hasn't it?"

"Yeah, we haven't been since our anniversary trip and that was three years ago. I want to visit her after her baby comes, but it's not really a good time right now."

"Why? Because of the restaurant? Darrin's the best sous chef around, he'd be fine. I can handle everything else." I swirl the water around my cup and pretend it's something stronger that could help the headache that's suddenly forming. "Walker doesn't need to babysit me."

"Come on, Wyatt." She tilts her head sympathetically. "Walker trusts you. So do I. You know that."

Did I know that?

She looks at me too closely, like she's somehow trying to convey the truth of her words and I think she does mean it. Right now. But there are things that just can't be forgiven and left in the past.

"Then why is it a bad time?"

She nibbles her bottom lip for a second. "Ugh, Walker would be so upset I was telling you this because we decided to keep it to ourselves for now, but I'm – "

"Pizza!"

We both jump at the loud voice booming down the hall.

"You startled me!" Ellie gasps with a huge smile on her face. It's been five years, and she still looks at him like she's seeing him for the first time.

It's nauseating.

"I got your pizza. The line was crazy," Walker says with a quick kiss on her lips. "I swear, one of these days you're going to have to broaden your horizons and get something that isn't pizza."

"You know it's just a craving," she argues as she follows him into the kitchen.

Walker shoots her a look and then looks at me.

"What did I do?" I ask, puzzled by the shocked look on his face.

"Nothing," Ellie says. "Walker's just dramatic." She takes a seat at the bar and opens the box. "Want some?"

"No, thanks, I got some food on my way over," I reply, unable to get the picture of the poor girl at the food truck out of my head.

I'd just finished my tacos when I saw her trying to move around the jerk that wouldn't get the hint. Everything about her body language was telling me she would rather be anywhere else, but men like that never care to pay attention to those kind of details.

I was about to walk away when I heard her defend herself and he still didn't care. I couldn't just leave her there alone, so I stepped in.

I didn't think much of it until she looked up at me behind her big round glasses. Now I can't seem to think about anything else.

"Don't tell me you got food from that taco truck again? Really, Wyatt, you have to expand your pallet every once and a while."

"I like those tacos," I defend myself. "And Daniel gives me a deal and only charges me for two but gives me four."

She chuckles as little feet come running down the hall and Lincoln screams, "Daddy!"

He runs through the sliding door and into the kitchen as fast as his little legs will carry him, which is pretty darn fast for such small things and jumps right into Walker's arms. Walker picks him up and immediately flips him upside down, tickling his stomach. Lincoln laughs his full, bright carefree laugh. It's my favorite sound in the world.

But it also hurts more than anything in the world.

Because only his dad can make him laugh like that.

"Put me down, I want pizza!"

He flails his little arms and giggles uncontrollably. Finally, Walker flips him right side up and sets him on the counter.

"It's all yours, buddy," Walker ruffles Lincoln's hair before taking a seat at the bar next to Ellie.

"Do you want to take some home, Wyatt. There's plenty. You can eat it tomorrow."

"Be quick, though. Dannie will have half of it gone before you can say 'pass the parmesan'."

I take in the scene as Walker catches Ellie's hand before her fist makes contact with his shoulder. He pulls her closer, resting her arm around his neck and kisses her cheek. She blushes with a silly smile on her face and Lincoln makes a mess of the pizza on the counter.

It's not until they're all laughing that I feel out of place and I stuff my hands in my pockets.

"It's okay, I got plenty of leftovers in the fridge I need to eat. I'll let myself out," I mumble as I make my way through the front door, closing it behind me as Lincoln's giggles start up again. The door shutting out the noise of the perfect, happy family.

I know I sound bitter, and I really have no right to be. I'm extremely lucky to have the relationship with Lincoln that I do considering all I put Ellie and Walker through.

I climb into my car and head to the restaurant instead of home. Something I find myself doing more and more lately. The restaurant isn't even open tonight, but there's something about it that feels different than my apartment. Even when the whole place is empty, it still feels occupied. It feels full. Unlike my apartment that feels like the bottom of a whiskey bottle after that last sip – hollow and cold.

I leave the radio off and listen to the soft purr of the engine, missing the loud gurgle of my old engine. The car's fairly new, only two years old. It's a good car and I needed a new one. Mine was barely running by the time I switched, but I miss it. It was the same one I had in college. It was filled with memories of all the late nights Ellie and I listened to crappy music while eating even crappier gas station snacks. All the memories I don't want to remember but can't stomach to forget.

I couldn't say when things fell apart or the moment everything changed. It happened slowly, one day at a time. One drink at a time that quickly turned into two, then three, before turning into so many I lost count. My mind so foggy

I didn't even know who I owed money to for whatever pills I bought on a weekly, sometimes daily, basis.

So many times I just want to forget and all the misplaced blame on the people who were better to me than I deserved.

She was patient with me. Looking back I see just how patient and understanding she was and wish she had walked out sooner. I used to think the day she walked out was the day my life changed, but it was long before that. That was just the day I realized what I'd done.

That's the day that sticks in my mind the most. The sound of the door slamming in my haze and how it knocked a picture of us off the bookshelf. The look on her face when she finally decided she was done. Those images engrained in my brain forever, reminding me just how much I've destroyed.

I mean it when I say I try not to dwell too much on the past. There's nothing in my past that I wish I still had and I'm not pining for relationships long lost. I'm not unhappy with where I am in my life right now, but I still regret how I got here.

I couldn't have gotten here without Walker. I'm lucky him and Ellie even let me stick around much less helped me get my feet back on the ground when I showed up after Lincoln's first birthday. I know it wasn't an easy decision for either of them. They've always put Lincoln first. Especially Walker. Ellie talks about all the gifts I bring and how my inability to ever say 'no' is my way of making up for lost time.

She's not wrong; that's exactly why I can never tell the kid no. But Walker's need to always be there and bring so much structure to the kid's life is his way of making up, too. We both feel like we've missed out on something, just in different ways.

Walker worries he'll never measure up as a dad.

I worry Lincoln will never know the truth.

That it should've been my name on that birth certificate.

chapter four
lucy

"Hey, Lucy Rae, can you make sure the Luther file gets sent to Bill?" my dad says with a light pat on my back as he walks into his office on Monday morning. "He called me on the way in and said he didn't get the details on the job."

"I sent it to him last week." I follow him into his office, stopping in the doorway. "I sent him an email *and* made a hard copy that I dropped off in their lockbox."

"He didn't get anything," he counters like he doesn't believe I sent it.

"He didn't get the email *or* hard copy?" I ask skeptically.

He doesn't look at me as he replies, "You know he's not good with emails."

Bill Foreman is our foreman. Yes, he's a foreman named Foreman. I'm still not sure I believe it. He's been our guy as long as I can remember, but he's getting older and slowly passing things off to his son, Jared.

"I'll email it again and copy Jared," I mumble as I drop myself back onto my desk chair just outside my dad's office. After I came back from college last year, I tried to move the desk to the other side of the room. I thought it looked better in the corner and it would be nice to see the front door as opposed to being right next to it and people startling me from behind as they entered. My dad, however, thought it was better to have me right outside his office for "easier communication." Because moving my desk ten feet to the west would make our communication so much worse.

"Can you drop off a hard copy as well?" he shouts through the open door.

I drop my face into my hands but shout back, "Sure thing."

I send the email quickly and type so forcefully, my keyboard shifts under my angry fingers, before printing the rest of the pages to drop off on my way home. Not that it's really on the way. I drove twenty minutes *out* of my way to drop them off four days ago.

"Can you come in here for a second, Lucy?"

I grab my blue binder and scurry into my dad's office for our standard Monday catch up. My father is a creature of habit. Most everyone is, but not like him. He eats the same breakfast of oatmeal with exactly six blueberries and a tablespoon of granola. He walks through the door every morning at exactly 8am. Not once in my life as he ever been late for a day of work. He goes golfing every Tuesday morning at six and meets my mom for lunch every Wednesday at the diner across the street. On Fridays, he works from home (I use the word 'work' loosely) and every Monday morning, he calls me into his office to go over the open accounts at 8:15, right after he gets his morning coffee.

"So what's going on?" he asks, taking a sip of his coffee as I take a seat across from him.

"Right," I open my binder and go through the updates on each account from the status on the glass panels we're waiting for to finish the Caldwell's 3.5-million-dollar home just outside the city, to the plumber finishing early on the Jefferson job. I detail everything as he listens on each account and the things that need immediate attention.

"Oh," I chime as I get to the end of my list. "We got a call from a Wyatt Reed." I flip the pages of my binder until I find the voicemail notes. "He owns *Abe's Place*. It's that fancy restaurant that opened a few years back on Route 9? They want to do some renovations and I guess they got a recommendation from the Brookes family."

His eyebrows pop up and he sits up a little straighter. "Brookes? I haven't heard that name in a while."

"Who is it?"

"Abe Brookes. He had a construction company. I was his foreman for years. He passed a long time ago. Car accident. It was horrible. His little girl was just eleven or twelve, I think, at the time." He nods toward my binder. "Who was the recommendation from?"

I check my notes again. "Not sure, he just said the Brookes family."

"Well, give him a call back and see what they want to do. If it's from the Brookes family, I want to be prompt about it."

Call him back? We've already bitten off far more than we can chew, and he wants to add another one?

"Dad, are you sure you want to take on more?" I ask carefully. "We're pretty swamped as it is." I clear my throat awkwardly. I never have been very good at confrontation when it comes to my dad. Vendors? Easy. Clients? Even easier. It's not hard for me to make business happen. I've been that way since I was a kid. Maybe it's from answering phone calls when I was fifteen. It's insane the things people will say to you when they have the phone between them and aren't looking you in the eye. I have thick skin. But with my dad, things are different. I mean, he's my dad. He gave me time-outs and took away my TV privileges when I talked back to him. It's harder to have a normal employee/boss relationship that's based on mutual respect.

"Maybe we should look at hiring someone part-time," I offer in a timid voice that even I can't take seriously.

He's shaking his head before I've finished. "We don't need help. We're doing fine."

I've brought up the idea of another hire for a while. Besides my uncle Matt, it's just me, my dad and my brother

Landon who are running everything in office. Logan and Luke were smart enough to opt out of the family business. My parents couldn't complain much when Logan decided to be a doctor and Luke went to law school. Overachievers ruining it for the rest of us.

My dad and Matt are the two main contractors and each have their own construction crew. I handle the paperwork side of things like booking appointments and writing up contracts and Landon is a combination of HR and Controller. When I graduated, Landon's wife got pregnant, and we started making plans for his paternity leave. The plans that just consisted of passing the majority of his responsibilities to me. Some things, Landon has to do being that only him or my dad can sign checks, so he comes in about once a week to do just what he needs to before dropping the rest on my desk as he walks out the door.

My dad has always worked by the philosophy that "too much business is good business." Often as a kid, he spent late nights in the office and weekends at different construction sites. He was rarely home.

I think that's part of why I wanted to work with him so bad as a teenager. I just wanted to spend time with him.

I want to argue and I open my mouth to try just one more time when he suddenly says, "Well, maybe you're right."

Huh?

"Things have picked up a bit," he goes on, oblivious to my shock. "Maybe we should look at hiring another manager to pick up the slack there."

Of course. He doesn't want to hire admin help, he wants to hire a project manager. Because all I'll ever be in his eyes is an assistant. No matter how much I do.

"Dad, project managers are expensive," I say tentatively. "I really think getting some part-time admin help would be enough."

"But we need help managing all the accounts."

Why do I have to spell it out? I take a deep breath and smile. "I could do that."

I try to sound confident, but it comes out as more of a question than demand.

His eyes widen, like this is new information to him. "You want to be a project manager?"

I nod slowly.

He shakes his head. "Lucy, you're too young."

My age? That's really what he's going with right now? Does he think I'm still seven?

"Daddy," I start. It's a low blow, but no matter how old a girl gets, she will always be looked at like a little girl to her parents. May as well take a little advantage while I still can. "I'm twenty-five. I can do this."

I give him the puppy dog eyes I've been using since I was a kid. The ones I know he can't say no to. Is this the professional direction I thought my life would go? No, it's not. I never thought I'd be begging my father for a professional title with my seven-year-old puppy dog eyes, but a girls got to do what a girls got to do.

He looks at me for a long time and I await the impending no. Time seems to stand still and I'm about to give up and admit defeat when he says, "Okay."

My eyes widen to saucers. "What?"

He chuckles a little at my reaction. "I said, okay."

"You mean I can be a project manager?"

He holds a hand up. "We'll see. Call the restaurant back and consider this your test project. If all goes well, we'll talk about a promotion and hiring an admin."

My heart is beating a million miles a minute and I have to repeat his words in my head four times before I can believe they're real.

"Thank you!" I beam as I run around the desk and wrap my arms around his neck. "I will be great, I promise. I'll reach out to him right now!"

He laughs. "Keep me updated on the project and we'll talk after."

"Yes, sir," I say as I grab my binder, bag, and bolt back to my desk.

After all the blood, sweat and tears I've given to this company, this is finally my shot to prove to my dad what I'm capable of.

I can do this.

chapter five

wyatt

Mr. Reed,

Thank you for your interest in Snow Better Builders. I'd love to meet at Abe's Place to discuss what you have in mind.

Does Wednesday at 9am work?
Looking forward to hearing from you,

L. Snow

It's a good start to a Monday morning, but I'm slightly irritated I got an email back instead of a phone call. I wanted to ask questions before we met. Like how much this contractor is going to cost us, for starters. I considered calling again to get my questions answered, but after two busboys called in sick and a pallet of lobster showed up at eight that we never ordered, I decided it wasn't worth it.

That's been the hardest part of the business world – learning when to keep quiet. Something Walker says I've improved on recently. I wasn't always so good at it. I picked fights often. With employees, coworkers, even vendors. When I first moved to town, I got in a fight with one of the busboys. I don't even remember what it was about, but I knocked him to the ground and broke his nose. I was going through serious withdrawals at the time. I relapsed the week before, and it didn't matter what anyone said or did, I was pissed. Walker promised me that night I had one last chance or I was out of their life for good. He even threatened a restraining order. I managed to get my crap together, but to this day I find myself struggling to keep my mouth shut.

If there is any contact I have to be careful with, though, it would be this one. Ellie's been raving about the Snow family nonstop, telling me about all the days she spent with her dad and how Nick Snow taught her to throw a punch.

I get a quick response back, confirming the time just as I'm walking into the kitchen.

"I'm meeting with the contractor Wednesday morning. Are you going to join?" I ask Walker, slipping my phone in my back pocket.

He doesn't look up from the stove when he asks, "What time?"

"Nine," I answer as one of the prep cooks pushes past me to get into the fridge. One of these days I should really remember his name. I'm pretty sure he's worked here for over a year.

"I can't," Walker responds. "Lincoln has music class."

"I thought he was playing soccer?"

"What? He can't be multi-faceted?"

My eyebrows come together. "Stop using big words you know I don't understand."

"Did we move the tomatoes?" Darren asks, popping up out of nowhere. "Hey Wyatt, what are you doing back here? I wasn't sure you even knew where the kitchen was."

"You're so hilarious Darren. You should remember I sign your checks."

He just chuckles and Walker interrupts us. "I put the tomatoes in the back of the fridge since we only make tomato soup once a week. It was in the way of everything else."

Darren bolts to the giant, bedroom-sized fridge and Walker turns back to me. "We're trying to give him options. I want him to know he can be anything. Just because he's good at soccer doesn't mean that's all he's good at or all he can do."

"He's five, Walker. What options does he need?"

"Setting the foundation early is important. Kids are vulnerable. If we tell him now that all he can do is soccer he's going to grow up believing it."

Add this to the list of reasons Walker's a much better dad than I ever would have been. I never would've thought things through this way. I would've made decisions as they came at me and not thought twice about the consequences. Just like I do with everything else in my life.

"Anyway, we're getting off topic," he says tossing a variety of vegetables in the pan. "I have to take Lincoln to music class tomorrow because Dannie has a doctor appointment. So, you'll have to handle this one on your own."

"Is Ellie okay?" I ask.

"Oh, yeah, she's fine. Just a check-up."

He doesn't look at me as he answers, and it has knots forming in my stomach. There's something he's not telling me.

"Check-up for what? You said she's fine, right?"

"Yeah, she's perfectly fine."

"Then why does she need a check-up?"

He sighs. "It's not a big deal, Wyatt. I promise, everything's fine."

"Then why are you being so secretive?"

"I'm not."

"Yes, you are. And Ellie was super weird when I was there on Friday. What's going on with you guys?"

He scowls at me out of the corner of his eye for a minute before he sighs and turns toward me, leaving the pan sizzling on the stove behind him. "She wanted to tell you anyway." He takes a deep breath and looks me directly in the eye. "Dannie's pregnant."

Out of all the horrible scenarios I'd run though in my head in the last ten seconds, not once did that thought cross my mind. Nothing could have prepared me for that bombshell.

My mouth falls open and I'm officially at a loss for words. A rarity for me. Ellie says I talk too much, though I'd argue that's the pot calling the kettle black. She never knows when to shut up. In this moment, though, I can't find a single word to say.

Ellie is pregnant. With Walker's kid.

I mean, of course it's Walker's kid, but still. Lincoln's going to have a brother. Or a sister.

"Wow," is all I can manage, my mouth suddenly very, very dry.

"We weren't going to tell anyone until she had her anatomy scan, but you're being nosy and all," he chuckles awkwardly.

"Congratulations," I say, surprising us both when I give him a hug.

"Thanks man," he says with a pat on my back before pulling away. "I'm really excited."

I run my suddenly clammy hands on my jeans. "When did you find out?"

"She told me after Lincoln's birthday party."

That was over two months ago. "How far along is she?"

"She'll be twenty weeks tomorrow. Her anatomy scan is scheduled for next Friday, but Mom and Winnie don't know yet. They might be coming down for Lincoln's game next weekend and we were gonna tell them then. So don't spill the beans. Oh and Lincoln doesn't know."

"My lips are sealed," I mumble. The thought passes in my brain that I have no idea what an anatomy scan is and he's said it twice. A reminder of how unfamiliar I am with pregnancy and all that goes along with it when I should know more than I do. I should definitely know more than Walker.

He eyes me for a moment, the food behind him ignored. "Are you okay?"

I nod. "Yeah, it's just...big news."

He nods once in agreement, eyeing me warily. "Yeah it is."

"I didn't know you guys were planning on having more kids. Especially at your age," I try to joke, but it falls flat.

He laughs halfheartedly. "Honestly, we didn't really plan it. We tried a little last year, but after a few tests the doctors said it was unlikely. This one was kind of a surprise."

I nod again unsure what else to do.

"You sure you're okay?"

"Yeah, man, I'm fine." I clear my throat, but the lump won't seem to go away. "I have some stuff to get together before tomorrow. So, uh, I'll just be in the office."

I don't wait for a response before I'm stomping down the back hallway and into the office.

Pregnant. Ellie is pregnant.

I shouldn't be having the reaction I am, but I don't know how to comprehend the reality that I'm in.

You think you've moved on, mended old wounds and then something crosses your path that rips it all open. Torn to shreds. Blood everywhere.

I drop myself into the office chair and try to remember pregnant Ellie. I only saw her twice when she was carrying Lincoln. Neither of them good visits. I was so high the last time I saw her before she had Lincoln, I hardly remember the visit.

I know she had a little nausea in the beginning, but it only lasted a couple weeks. She always craved pizza and couldn't sit down for long periods of time or her feet would swell till she couldn't get her shoes on.

All the things I've heard over the years of how her pregnancy with Lincoln went, but none of it did I experience firsthand. But now she's pregnant. And I'm somehow trapped in the life I should've lived all those years ago.

I wonder if her cravings will be the same and then I remember that she wanted pizza on Saturday night after the game. Just like with Lincoln. No wonder the kid's obsessed with pizza.

I try to push aside all the raveling emotions and focus on the contractor. I wanted to send the floor plan of the restaurant and a brief overview of what we want to do before the meeting, hoping to speed up the process.

The computer freezes on my email as it does more often than not. I keep telling Walker we need a new one, but he's a cheapskate and always has been.

Until he was dropping money in your hand like candy when you didn't deserve it.

The knot in my stomach tightens.

It's an odd feeling, regret. It tastes sour and feels like you've been a punching bag for hours on end. It's not that I wish I was with Ellie. Her and Walker are perfect for each other and they're the best parents to Lincoln.

I just wish things could be different.

I wish I had a drink in my hand.

chapter six
lucy

"He looks like a serial killer."

Jenny swipes down on yet another man. Or boy as she calls them because according to her, "None of these unwashed infants have the emotional or mental maturity to be considered men."

She swipes down on two more immediately and I laugh. "You think everyone looks like a serial killer."

"Because everyone does!" She turns her phone toward me so I can see the picture on the screen. "Who tucks their flannel into their jeans? Serial killers!"

She's not totally wrong on this guy. The tucked in flannel with the handlebar mustache is kind of sending serial killer vibes.

"Do you even look at the things they write on their profile?" I ask.

She scoffs. "Honey, if they don't have the face, what's the point of the chase?"

I laugh once. "Where in the world did that saying come from?"

"Years and years of horrendous experience." She tosses her phone across the couch. "What about you? When was the last time you checked your profile?"

"The day I set it up. Or should I say, the day *you* set it up."

Jenny coerced me into creating an online dating profile about six months ago. It was two in the morning and we were high on sugar and vampire movies. I agreed and matched with a few people, but once I was coherent enough in the morning to realize what I'd done, I never responded to any of the messages. I choose to pretend it doesn't exist. Jenny, however, refuses to let that happen.

"How long has it been since you've been on a date?"

"A while," I admit.

"Was the last date that one your mom set you up on with the pharmacist?"

I throw my head back with a groan. "Ugh, don't remind me. He was so boring."

She picks up my phone and wiggles it in front of my face. "I'm sure you have lots of messages on the app if you'd just check it."

I would love to date someone. If I didn't have to go through the horrid dating experience. I know that sounds like a contradiction, but after a while, boring small talk over crappy dinners gets old. And they rarely turn into anything. First dates are only fun, well, the first time.

I snatch my phone out her hands. "I'm focusing on my career right now." It's a lame excuse because one could argue being an administrative assistant isn't exactly a career, but it's the start of one. At least, I'm hoping it is.

"Not the career excuse again." She groans. "You should've gotten that guy's phone number at the food truck?"

"Daniel?"

She rolls her eyes. "Not the actual food truck guy, gosh. The sexy stranger that saved you from the pervert."

I'd be lying if I hadn't thought the exact same thing multiple times the last week. He was so kind to me, a complete stranger as Jenny pointed out. He didn't have to do what he did. And I'd also be lying if I said he wasn't the most beautiful person I'd ever laid eyes on in real life. It was embarrassing how many dreams had revolved around him since our chance encounter. I didn't even know his name and I was dreaming about him sweeping me off my feet almost every night.

"And when, exactly, would I have gotten his phone number? He wasn't hitting on me anyway, he was just being nice."

"Men aren't just *nice.* They all have a motive. And most of those motive are getting into – "

"Gross, no." I cut her off. "You really got to get off the dating apps if you think that's the motive of most men."

"Tell me about it," she mumbles. "But seriously, that was a total meet-cute and you just ruined it.

"A meet-cute?"

"Ugh, you have got to read more." She adjusts herself to a seating position on the couch. "A meet-cute is how you and the love of your life meet in, like, a totally organic, only-fate-could've-done-this kind of way."

"You think fate brought that man to the food truck on a Sunday night and is the love of my life? Pretty sure an empty stomach and the inability to cook is most likely what brought him to the food truck."

"The way to a man's heart is through his stomach. Fate knew what he was doing."

"Oh goodness gracious, you're insane. Now if you don't mind I'm going to get back to more important things in life."

"Okay, fine, we can talk about boring things. Are you ready for tomorrow?"

I smile. "Couldn't be more ready."

I got an email back from Wyatt Reed confirming he could meet at nine in the morning and a following email that had more details than I could've dreamed. He sent me the floor plan for the restaurant and even sent a rough draft of what they were looking to do. It was a simple sketch that looked like it was drawn with sharpie on a napkin, but I got the idea. He gave me their budget and timeline expectations, all of which can easily be done.

I had to confirm with my dad three times today to make sure I hadn't dreamed our entire conversation, and that I was, in fact, leading this project. He just laughed and said, "Do your worst, Lucy Rae."

Thankfully, luck has been on my side with this one. With so many details up front from the client, I was able to email a few of the architects we recommend early this morning and get some renderings drawn up quickly. A few owe me some favors that I was more than eager to cash in.

"Why don't you show him one of your designs?" Jenny asks as I organize the sketches in my binder. "I saw the stuff you were working on last night. It's good."

I'm shaking my head vigorously. "I can't. There's a lot riding on this project. I have to prove to my dad I can do this."

I drew up some sketches last night because I needed something to relax my mind, not because I had any intention of actually showing the client. I'm not a real architect and throwing my amateur sketches into the stack would be unprofessional.

"What exactly do you have to prove that you haven't already? You've basically been the head project manager for over a year."

"Yes, but this time he's actually acknowledging it," I argue.

"What does that have to do with showing your designs, though? You should show this guy."

"Jenny, no." I pull them out and drop them on the table. "It's just doodles. This is a really important project. I have to take it seriously."

"What was the point of all the insane hours you spent at the beginning of the year studying for that stupid test if you aren't going to use your license?"

"Just because I'm licensed, doesn't mean I'm reputable yet."

"And how does one become reputable, exactly?"

I shoot her a glare.

"Won't you have to give him a few samples before he picks an architect? He doesn't have to know one of the sketches in the pile is yours." She reaches for the papers again.

"No!" I practically yell and she drops them on the table.

"Fine, don't listen to me. But don't come crying to me when you grow old and die in your dad's office chair, his ashes on the desk next to you since you could never cut ties."

"Could you be more dramatic?" I raise my eyebrows.

She shrugs one shoulder as she twirls a piece of auburn hair around her finger. "Probably."

"Go away." I chuck a crumbled-up paper at the back of her head as she scurries into her room and shuts the door behind her.

Jenny and I are complete opposites in pretty much every way possible. She never takes no for an answer and is always trying something new. Last year she went skydiving because she had a random whim on a Saturday morning that it would be fun. She talks loudly without embarrassment and tells people what she thinks no matter the consequences. She's afraid of nothing and it shows. I've never seen someone who truly doesn't care what anyone thinks of them.

Me, I hate causing drama and talk way too much. I follow the rules and don't ask questions, not wanting to cause trouble. I've spent my entire life being Little Lucy Rae who does whatever she's asked. Which has ultimately led to me doing what everyone else wants and ignoring my own desires.

But she's wrong about this job. This is just the beginning. My dad will see all I can do and who knows what doors it could open for me.

I turn my attention back to my laptop and try to organize the portfolio. Most of it is already done with a template I reuse for every client, but this one has to be the best I've ever presented. I check the time and it's already past midnight. I should sleep, but I've only proofread it twice. Everyone knows third times the charm.

I put the finishing touches on the pitch as I proofread for the third and final time, compiling all our contacts and vendor list along with the few sketches I was able to get from the top architects in the city. I print everything out and make a neat stack on the table, color coded with tabs for each section. I can't help but glance back at my design every few seconds, Jenny's words in my mind.

I've always loved architecture. I couldn't decide when I applied to NYU what I loved more, so I picked both. I loved my architecture classes so much and sometimes wished it was my major, but I don't regret the choices I've made.

There's always been a small part of me that's wanted to ask my dad about showing my sketches to clients, but he can't even agree to give me a promotion, much less this.

It would be easy to slip that paper I worked on for hours into the folder. He probably wouldn't even pick the design so where's the harm?

The harm is he could hate it. And that's a chance I'm just not ready to take.

chapter seven
wyatt

I'm late.

I'm always late. I can hear Walker's voice in my head chastising me for never taking anyone else's time into consideration.

I do try, but it's hard sometimes. Especially with the morning I've had. I slept straight through my alarm and woke up ten minutes before I needed to leave. I took the quickest shower of my life, ran my hand through my hair and bolted out the door. And then of course there was an accident getting out of the neighborhood because Mr. Brinkley on the corner always parks his car too close to the stop sign so people tend to run into it when they take the turn too quickly. I can't even count how many times he's had to replace his bumper since I moved in.

I miss the city.

I blame Winnie for my tardiness. My older sister tends to call at the worst times. I failed to put my phone on silent and woke up at midnight to the sound of her phone call. I think she calls after her kids are in bed, but often times forgets the two-hour time difference since they moved to Illinois last year. I don't know what time I finally hung up, but I'll blame her for missing my alarm and showing up fifteen minutes late.

As I pull into the parking lot, I see a small grey sedan parked in the front parking spot, so I pull up next to it hoping he hasn't been waiting long.

It's not until I have the car in park that I do a double take as I spot the petite woman with short blonde hair and a tight black skirt standing in front of the door in stilettos, blue binder held close to her chest.

Who could that be?

I climb out of the car slowly. "Can I help you?"

"Are you Wyatt Reed?" she asks in a soft voice.

"Yes."

She takes a few small steps until she's at the edge of the curb standing in front of me. She extends her hand out and offers a wide grin.

"I'm the project manager from *Snow Better Builders*."

I think I might be dreaming. Especially since I've been dreaming about those blue eyes for the last two weeks.

It's the girl from the food truck. The girl that has occupied far too many thoughts in the last week considering I talked to her for approximately three minutes.

Does she recognize me? She extended her hand and introduced herself as if we haven't ever met before. Though, you could argue we haven't met before; I never did get her name. I highly doubt it affected her as much as it affected me anyway. For her it was just a kind gesture from a stranger that she'll probably never think of again.

I stare at her for an unbelievable amount of time before I process what she just said.

There is no way this...this, *girl*, is the contractor. She's small in every way. Even with her high heels and the extra two inches from the curb, she just reaches my nose. I'm pretty sure my hand could wrap completely around her waist. Her neck is slender and her lips perfectly plump. Her hair is straight as a pin, pushed back behind one ear. Even her ears are small.

Her eyes, though, are anything but small. They're wide and eager as they stare into mine behind her big round glasses. I have to clear my throat to pull myself out of them.

"Sorry," I shut my car door and take her hand, shaking it once. It's half the size of mine and I worry I'll break it if I'm not careful. "I was just...expecting someone else."

"A man?" she asks, pulling her hand from mine with a little attitude, like she's been through this a million times before.

"Well, yeah," I say awkwardly.

"Everyone usually is."

Suddenly a few things click together in my head. "Is that why you didn't call back, but emailed?"

She nods once.

"And why you didn't sign your first name?"

"I've learned people are much more likely to meet with me when they don't hear my voice on the other end of the phone or see a female name at the bottom of an email," she says with her shoulders back and head held high. Though, I can't imagine anyone not calling her back.

Her voice sounds like silk.

"I have a feeling if they saw you, they'd feel differently," I quip before I can think better of it. Probably not the best idea to flirt with the contractor.

"I'm not interested in lewd comments, Mr. Reed."

A lot of sass for someone so small. I don't think I've ever had someone turn me down so fast. The crooked grin usually gets them pretty quick. "You're right," I hold my hands up in apology. "I'm sorry. Come on in, I'll show you around."

I hold the door open for her and she walks in confidently and makes her way into the middle of the room like she owns the place. She stands in the center of the dining room, circling slowly. It's a pretty open space, something Walker felt very passionate about before we opened. He didn't want there to be little walking space. He wanted plenty of room between each table and not a bunch of walls separating everyone. When you first walk in, it looks more like a reception hall than a restaurant. With the lights strung on the ceiling, it feels like it too. It's that personal, slightly fancy touch that brings people back. At least, that's what Ellie says.

Miss Snow's eyes scan slowly as she turns in a full circle until she's seen every piece. Then she begins to move. She walks the perimeter of the room before walking through each table, touching on every nook and cranny. I don't think she misses a single speck of dust or chipped paint on the wall. She remains silent as she wanders from one side to the other. Her eyebrows are pushed together in concentration as she lightly nibbles on the tip of her pen cap.

Pen chewing shouldn't be so enticing.

Her hair is short, barely brushing her shoulders, as she moves around the dining room. Her features are delicate and her skin flawless. She looks young. Early twenties maybe. She walks a little faster across the room, her chin tilted to examine the ceiling. Her hips sway involuntarily in the tight black skirt that touches just above her knees and I mentally slap myself for even noticing.

She's the contractor for crying out loud.

Thankfully, she breaks the silence.

"There's a lot to work with here, but the room is small. I believe it was the south side you wanted to expand, correct?" she asks as she moves toward the far right side of the building running her perfectly polished, bright red fingers over the windowsill.

I clear my throat. "How old are you?"

She stops suddenly and turns her eyes on me. "Excuse me?"

"I'm sorry, I just – "

"Old enough," she protests with her nose in the air.

I raise a quizzical brow.

"With all due respect, Mr. Reed, my age is irrelevant."

"Wyatt."

"What?"

"Mr. Reed is unnecessary," I argue, shoving my hands into my pockets. "You can just call me Wyatt."

Her eyes narrow. "Noted."

"And your name?"

"Miss Snow."

My smile widens.

Her scowl deepens.

I laugh once. "You're not as soft as you look, are you?"

She crosses her arms as she retorts, "I didn't realize I looked soft."

"You're what? Five-feet tall?"

She stands a little taller, pushing her glasses up her nose with her index finger. "Five-foot-five. And a half. Which makes me above average."

That's an understatement.

We stare each other down for a moment before she sighs and her shoulders drop slightly, her arms falling to her sides. "Look, Mr. Reed. I realize I may have led you to believe some things that weren't exactly true. For that, I apologize. But I've been working for *Snow Better Builders* for a long time and I can do this job and do it well. I hope you won't make any snap judgements that would take your business elsewhere."

Her attitude is gone and she looks almost nervous. I wonder how many times she's been turned away for reasons completely out of her control.

"Of course not," I say with a wave of my hand. "I shouldn't have asked your age. It was unprofessional, you're right."

She sighs in what I assume is appreciation and I stick my hand out for her. "Let's start over. I'm Wyatt."

She laughs lightly and places her soft palm in mine. "Miss Snow."

I scoff as I reluctantly release her hand and motion toward the table. "All right then, Miss Snow, we can sit? Unless you'd like to look around some more."

"No, sitting is good."

She brushes past me and a faint smell of fruit invades my senses.

She's the contractor, man. Get it together.

chapter eight
lucy

So, Mr. Reed is Wyatt.

And Wyatt, as Jenny has been calling him, is my beautiful prince that saved me from misfortune.

In his voicemail, he sounded much, *much* older. To be honest, I'm surprised I didn't recognize his voice on the phone. Seeing as I've had the timbre of his voice burned into my memory, unable to forget the way it made my insides turn.

He looks younger than I remember. Granted, it was dark on Main Street and his beard was much thicker. He must've just shaved this morning. He can't possibly be a day over thirty. He asked me my age like he couldn't believe I was old enough to be here and it took everything in me not to ask the same question. He doesn't look even remotely old enough to have a business so successful it's expanding.

I sit at the table he motions to and open my binder trying not to be hurt by the fact that he didn't recognize me.

Guess that night wasn't that big of a deal to a man that probably saves twenty women a week. It's probably his move. I'm sure he wanders around town waiting for women to be caught in uncomfortable circumstances and he's there, waiting to swoop in and save the day.

Okay, I doubt he's that pathetic, but I have to make myself feel a little better about the fact that the man I talked to for maybe a minute that has consumed far too many thoughts in the last two weeks doesn't even recognize me.

"I went through the details you emailed, which were extremely helpful, by the way," I start as I pull the floor plans out and lay them on the table in front of him. "Because of that, I was able to get a few plans drawn up. These are some of the best architects in the city."

He takes the first one and looks at it carefully, analyzing every bit of it.

"My personal favorite is the first one. He is, by far, the best architect in town. He's local. Lives not too far from here, actually. I had to pull a few strings to get a mock up from him so quickly, but thanks to the floor plans you sent me he was able to get it done. It's a bit rough since he was in a rush, but he's worth it. Trust me."

He nods absently as he sets the sketch aside and moves on to the next. "I believe you mentioned you're looking to cut out the whole south side of the parking lot, correct? Wanting to add room for at least ten more tables?"

"Yeah," he mumbles as he scans the page.

"What are your plans for parking? If we cut out that half of the parking lot, how are you going to have parking for ten more tables?"

"We got the land next door. They're tearing down the building and we bought the land. We're going to merge it into our parking lot."

"Oh, that's great!" I respond as he moves onto the next drawing. "That was the one thing I wasn't clear on with what you sent over. I was – " I cut short when I notice the page he's holding. The one I know for a fact I left on the kitchen counter yesterday as to not mix it up with all the others. My eyes widen as he scans over every tiny detail.

There's a small sticky note on the back with Jenny's handwriting.

Knock him dead. If those heals don't, these drawings sure will ;) Don't be embarrassed of your talents. You deserve this.

I snatch the paper out of his hands so fast it tears slightly, and his eyes practically jump out of his skull.

"Sorry," I stumble as I try to shove the paper back into my binder, but all I do is crinkle it, tearing it even more. "So sorry. This wasn't supposed to be in here. This wasn't one of the options."

"I liked that one."

I stop my horrendous bunching of the paper and stare at him like a deer in the headlights. "What?"

He points to the crumbled ball in my hand. "I like that one. The curved design in the window is really cool."

"Really?"

He smiles and his teeth peek out just enough to tease me and make me want more. "Yeah. I mean, we might have to get some good blinds cause the sun will shine right through that window at dinner time."

I shake my head. "The sun rises and sets east to west. The rounded window would be on the south side of the building. It would be fine with just some light-filtering blinds."

"I guess the architect would've thought of that, huh?" His eyes practically shimmer as he rests his forearms on the table and leans closer.

"Yeah, they did." I mumble. His eyes are extremely dark. Almost black they're so brown except for a little circle of gold around the iris. It's surprisingly intoxicating.

Why am I looking at his eyes this closely?

"Well, what else you got for me?"

"Got for you?" I ask breathlessly. Do all men smell this good? I'm not sure. It's been so long since I've been so close to one.

He smirks a little and points to the table. "Yeah, in your binder."

"Binder," I say sitting up straight, blinking away my unacceptable lack of professionalism.

Pull yourself together, Lucy!

"Yes, well, uh, construction wise, we have our own in-house personnel for that. As far as everything else, we contract with all the vendors. You won't have to worry about anything. Just pick the design you want, and we'll make it happen."

He's still smiling and the air in the room feels thicker than it was before. Suddenly, I find myself stumbling over my words.

"We'll have to discuss bathroom expansion. You know, cause the current ones are pretty small. Only two stalls according to the floor plans you sent. I mean, there isn't much room in the current location to expand unless you want to take space from the kitchen, which is a terrible idea. I think we could add a second bathroom closer to the front, maybe? Not a full bathroom with multiple stalls, but maybe a family bathroom option? Granted, if you plan on adding ten more tables, you're gonna need more urinals."

I laugh awkwardly at my ridiculous joke and internally cringe that I actively chose to say the word 'urinal' out loud in a business meeting with a total stranger.

"Yes, we wouldn't want to forget about the urinals," he replies with a half-smile and I can feel my face turn beet red. He eyes my cheek for just a moment before he clears his throat. "So where do we go next?"

"Bedroom," I blurt, eyes wide as saucers at my mistake. "I mean, bathroom! We should look at the *bathroom* and see where we want to expand. You know, for the urinals."

Oh my gosh, Lucy, stop saying urinal.

He's trying not to laugh and I want to shrivel up like a grape and be fed to a dying fish. That would be more pleasant than this conversation.

I was so prepared for this meeting. I put on my best outfit, I straightened my hair and I had everything organized. This was going to be my best pitch I've ever done in my whole darn life and it's turning into a disaster all because Mr. Flirty McPerfect Eyes won't stop smiling. And I'm pretty that's a dimple on his left cheek that keeps teasing me.

Maybe Jenny's right, it's been too long since I've been on a date. Even longer since I kissed a man.

Why am I thinking about kissing right now?

"Sure," he says with the same subtle grin. "Lead the way, boss."

He stands next to me and even in my heels he's a head taller than me. My parents are short people, my dad's only five-eight. I didn't have much hope in that department. Hence the heels. People don't take you as seriously when you're this small and I take every precaution to prevent people from making snap judgements.

Wyatt was right, I didn't call back for a reason. After a few 'no, thank yous' over the phone you learn quickly that people in this industry expect men.

I learned long ago to stop signing my emails with my name and avoiding phone conversations until the contracts were signed. Call it sexist, but it is what it is. I've learned to adapt.

"Right," I respond a little too loudly and he chuckles softly. I wonder if I could make him do that again. I've never heard a man laugh like that. So...deep.

"Let's go," I sputter a little too loudly. I take a deep breath and do my best to exude confidence as we go over the different options for bathroom locations and yes, how many urinals. I don't even say anything awkward, which is a real feat. I show him a couple of the designs again as we meander through the restaurant and the different ideas from each architect.

After about an hour, we find ourselves at the table we started.

"So," I ask laying the papers on the table. "Any of the designs stand out to you?"

"I like the last option the best."

I look up at him. "What?"

He reaches past the designs I laid neatly on the table for the one I left crumbled in a ball. He opens it carefully and tries to straighten it out. "Those are great, but I really like this one. The rounded window is really nice and I like how it pulls everything together. That corner space in the back has always just kind of been there, but I like the way it's been incorporated into the dining room with the private room option. We've never really known what to do with that."

"Yeah, it could be used for private reservations."

"That's a great idea! I love it," he smiles and my heart skips. Literally, figuratively, I have no idea, but something is going on in my chest that I can't put a name to.

"You want to use this architect?" I marvel, holding up my design.

He nods.

"You're sure?"

"Positive."

I'm not sure what to say as he stares at me. I must look like an idiot ogling my design with my mouth hanging open in shock. I'm saved by the bell when his phone rings.

"It's my brother. Sorry," he mutes the call and puts it back in his pocket.

"You can take it. I have what I need. I'll just get the contract written up and send it to you to look at, if that's all right?"

"Sounds good."

"Great," I say as I gather everything back into my bag. "It was great meeting you, Mr. Reed."

"It's just Wyatt, please," he says, all joking gone.

"Wyatt," I repeat and he smiles.

I rarely tell clients my first name. It's already difficult to get them to take me seriously for all the aforementioned reasons, but asking them to call me Miss Snow creates an immediate expectation of professionalism and I've seen it work more than once.

But there's something about his crooked grin and dark eyes boring into mine that has me saying, "You can call me Lucy."

His smile widens, heaven help me. "I look forward to seeing you again, Lucy."

chapter nine
wyatt

"Why are you so happy?" Walker asks as I walk into his kitchen later that afternoon.

"What do you mean?"

"You're smiling."

"So? I smile all the time," I argue as I grab a water out of his fridge.

He scoffs. "No, you don't. You never smile. What happened today?"

I take a seat on a barstool as he turns back to the stove. "I smile."

"No, you mope."

"I do not mope."

"Answer the question."

I shrug. "It was just an ordinary day."

That couldn't be further from the truth. It was anything but ordinary. Lucy was anything but ordinary.

I left that meeting unsure how to navigate the thoughts and feelings swirling through my mind. Mixing this professional with the stranger I haven't been able to stop thinking about.

Never in my thirty-five years of life have I ever been so enthralled with a woman. Something I don't admit lightly. She went through every detail, missing nothing. She was incredibly smart and proved me wrong in thinking she was too young. She stood tall, despite her short stature and made me feel small. Not in a belittling kind of way, but in a kind of way that made me know she's capable of so much more than you'd think.

He raises an eyebrow but doesn't push any further. "Did you meet with the contractor?"

"Yeah."

"Do you think he'll be good?"

I clear my throat. "She, actually. It was a woman."

"Oh, okay. Was she good?"

"Yeah, she was pretty young, but she's super smart. She had some great ideas and was extremely thorough. She already sent me the contract. She took her time and..." I trail off as he turns around and smirks at me. "What?"

"Well, that makes more sense now."

"What makes more sense?"

"Your drool."

"What are you even talking about?"

He crosses his arms across his chest and leans against the counter. "I'm guessing she was pretty."

"Excuse me?"

He laughs once. "You're blushing."

"I am not *blushing*," I roll my eyes as I take a swig of water.

"You thought she was hot."

I choke on the water. "Walker, it was a business meeting."

He just chuckles.

"I mean, she wasn't ugly by any means, but..."

"Right," he nods with an obnoxious grin.

"Shut up, man." I nod toward the stove. "Isn't it a little early for dinner?" It's only two o'clock.

He laughs at the abrupt change of topic and turns back to the stove as he replies, "I like to make it early sometimes for Dannie and Lincoln before I head to the restaurant."

"What are you making?"

"Steak medallions with mashed potatoes."

"Oh, my favorite," Ellie walks into the kitchen sniffing strongly. "Smells so good!"

"Winnie called last night," I say quickly, changing the subject. The last thing I need in my life is Ellie's opinions on my love life. It's her favorite topic these days. A few months ago she randomly asked me if I'd gone out with anyone recently. It was so out of nowhere, I stumbled over my words, and she took that has me saying 'help me'. She's tried to set me up a few times, but I've been lucky enough to evade any potential meet ups.

I haven't really dated anyone since college. I mean, there's been a few women here and there, but nothing serious. When I first decided to get clean, I cut off women. My sponsor told me I needed to worry about myself before I could add a woman to the mix and he wasn't wrong. I had a lot I needed to work through. Once I hit my year mark he recommend I put myself out there again. Whatever that means. I took a few women out, some even lasting two or three dates. However, besides a few dinners, a couple coffee shops, and some alone time in the back of my car, nothing really happened with any of them. The few things that did happen I'm not proud of in the least.

I've been focused on other things. Better things. Like getting myself together and being there for Lincoln and my family. I haven't had any time for dating.

It's not that I've completely cut women off, I'm just not so sure a relationship is even possible anymore. Not after all the choices I've made.

I've told Ellie as much, trying to convey the feelings I don't quite understand, but I know she just wants me to be happy. I think there's a part of her that still feels guilty. Guilt she shouldn't carry considering anything that did or did not happen between us is my fault and my fault alone.

"You talked to Winnie? What'd she say?" Walker asks, not looking away from his dinner.

"Said they can't come this weekend, but probably next month. Said she would call mom and they'd work out a time together."

"Yeah, she's been wanting to come for one of Lincoln's soccer games and bring the kids."

"I texted her his schedule last week," Ellie adds. "I did not, however, send it to your mother."

Ellie and my mother have a very interesting relationship. My mom likes her, she just likes to give her a hard time. And Ellie isn't exactly what one would call patient.

Walker chuckles. "You know Mom loves you."

"She's never forgiven me for the wedding."

"Yes, she has."

"Really?" Ellie says with raised eyebrows, tossing her hair behind her. "Then why is it that every single time she comes over she makes a comment about it?"

"Can you blame her?" I add.

Her eyes shoot daggers at me.

"Come on, you got married at the courthouse. With a six-month-old baby. In a purple dress."

"It was the exact wedding I wanted," she argues. "We wanted it to be small. It was a perfect day."

"Yeah, I'm sure cleaning poop out of a car seat and your dress was exactly how you wanted to spend your wedding night," I joke. I wasn't there, of course, but I've heard the story. The second they walked out of the courthouse, Lincoln had a complete blowout that went up his back, out the sides all over Walker's white shirt and Ellie's purple dress. They didn't have the diaper bag. They argued about who was supposed to grab it the whole way home over Lincoln's screams.

Walker turns around to drain the boiled potatoes. He places the pot in the sink as he wraps an arm around Ellie's waist. "The night got better," he murmurs as he presses a kiss to her temple and she giggles. Ellie giggles. Never in all the years we spent together in college did Ellie ever *giggle.*

"Gross," I mutter as I take a swig of the sparkling water. I could really use something stronger if I have to sit through their insufferable PDA.

"It was the exact wedding I wanted," she says again as Walker turns back to the stove. "Why would I want to wear white? It's so boring. At least purple has some pizazz. And why does your mother care what color I wore? She was invited, wasn't she? Besides, the pictures looked amazing."

I laugh once. She's not wrong. The pictures are amazing. Lincoln and Walker wore purple bow ties to match Ellie's dress. Purple shouldn't have been a surprise. I've never seen Ellie wear something as simple as white. She's always in some combination of colors you'd never think would go together, but somehow it works for her.

My mom and Ellie's grandma went to the courthouse wedding, but that was the end of the guest list. Even Winnie wasn't invited. Walker got an earful about that later. My mom took the pictures with her phone, but they looked perfect. You'd never know it was just the five of them in a stuffy courthouse room.

"Whatever. Moving on," Ellie says as she snags something off Walker's pan and he swats her hand away. "I heard Walker kept his mouth shut for all of five seconds and spilled the beans."

"The baby beans?" I ask.

"Yes, the baby beans that he insisted we keep sealed nice and tight until I was twenty weeks. Which was ridiculous, I'm already showing."

Now that she points it out, I can't unsee it. She's wearing baggy overalls, but I can still see her belly protruding just a bit. You wouldn't notice unless you were looking for it. Now I know why she's been wearing baggy t-shirts and her overalls every day. She was trying to hide it.

"Well, I thought – " Walker attempts to defend himself, but Ellie interrupts.

"He went on and on to me about how we shouldn't tell anyone and make sure everything is good before spreading it around, and then was upset that I almost told you the other day because he wanted to be the one to say it himself." She gives him a stink eye and he points at me. "Wyatt has a crush."

Ellie's eyes go wide with excitement, her annoyance at Walker completely forgotten. I scowl at his back. "Thanks, man."

"My pleasure," he says with a satisfied grin, happy to not be the brunt of Ellie's anger.

"I do not have a crush."

"Yes, you do."

I toss a boiled piece of potato at the back of his head that just mushes into his hair.

"Who is she?"

"The contractor," Walker says, wiping the potato away.

"Contractor? You have a crush on Nick Snow?" Ellie looks at me.

I roll my eyes. "No, his daughter, Lucy."

"So you admit you have a crush?" Walker chimes.

"Heaven help me with you two," I groan. "Lucy is managing the renovations, but I don't have a crush on her. So, take that mischievous look off your face, Ellie."

Her features turn even more coy. "Lucy's cute."

Cute is too small a word.

"You've met her?"

She shakes her head. "Not in person. But they still send me a Christmas card every year."

Walker adds, "I knew the name sounded familiar when you told me."

I take another drink of the sparkling water and pretend it's something much, much stronger. "There are a lot of pretty girls in the world that are not our contractor." They may be pretty, but I doubt they're that beautiful. I cough awkwardly. "Besides, she's practically a kid."

Walker scoffs. "Do you even know how old she is?"

"I'd guess like nineteen. Maybe twenty if I'm stretching it."

"I think she's twenty-four or twenty-five," Ellie adds. "I remember when her dad took paternity leave. I was like nine or ten. It was a whole mess. My dad had to jump in and was super busy all the time. I spent a lot of time with him around then."

"See?" Walker says. "She's twenty-five. Not eighteen.

"What's the difference?"

"Seven years," Ellie jokes and I shoot her an annoyed glare. "Walker's eight years older than me."

"Yeah, eight years, not ten."

"What's two years? I mean, she's managing a pretty big project. She's not a child."

"You don't even know this girl," I say. "Why are you trying so hard to set us up?"

"I know her family. Or I used to. My dad really relied on Nick Snow for a lot of things. He came to my dad's funeral," her voice drops slightly as it always does when she talks about her dad and Walker gives her arm a squeeze. "They're good people. I don't know Lucy personally, but I'm sure she's just as incredible as the rest of them."

"Why are we talking like this?" I ask. "She's our contractor. I met her all of one time." That they know of. You can bet I'll be keeping the food truck incident to myself. "To go over the renovations. This is completely unprofessional," I say more to myself than anyone else. "I'm surprised the two of you don't agree."

"You're right," Walker nods. "It's better to keep things professional. The last thing we need is to complicate anything. You're being very mature about this, Wyatt."

"Thank you," I sigh and look at Ellie.

"Don't look at me. Maturity is overrated. I say go for it. You haven't been this flustered in...well, ever."

"I'm not flustered," I groan. "Why do I spend so much time here? I'm going home."

"Let us know how things go!" Ellie calls as I walk through the front door.

Nothing's going anywhere. For a lot of reason. First and foremost, because this is business and I've worked hard to get where I am in my career. Second, because the last time I got close to someone, I screwed up both our lives.

I'm not doing that again.

chapter ten
lucy

"Jenny! You will never believe what happened!" I yell as I burst into the apartment.

"Girl, I don't have that kind of energy right now," she groans from the couch. "Tone it down." Her feet are propped on the coffee table, her arm draped over her forehead with her hair in a messy bun.

"Well, you're going to have to tone it *up*, because he picked my design!" I squeal as I plop down next to her.

"Okay, go slower, I'm lost. Who picked your what?"

"Wyatt Reed picked my design!"

"A man?" she bolts up right. She adjusts herself, tucking her feet beneath her and turns toward me. "Tell me everything. Who is Wyatt Reed?"

I roll my eyes. "He own's the restaurant, *Abe's Place.* I met with him this morning."

"Oh right," she smirks. "So, he saw your design."

"Yes! And normally I would be really, *really* mad at you for doing that," I smack her in the arm, "but I can't be because he picked it!"

"Is he cute?"

"What?"

"You heard me."

"Jenny, he's a client. I didn't even notice what he looked like," I lie through my teeth. I could hardly focus on anything except how beautiful he was. "I didn't even notice. I was trying to get a contract signed."

"Liar. You're flushed," she says, waggling her eyebrows. "He was hot, wasn't he? The name Wyatt Reed just screams sex appeal."

I shoot her a side-eyed glare. "I think Janice may be right, you do need a man."

"That's the meanest thing you've ever said to me," she deadpans.

I laugh once and hug the pillow so tight I'm surprised the seams don't pop. "He picked my design, Jenny. I'm going to see my own work come to life for the first time."

"That's amazing, Lucy, I'm really excited for you." She rubs my arm encouragingly.

"I know. I don't even know what to do next, this is so crazy." The adrenalin is still pumping, and I feel like I'm out of breath. He picked my design. I gave him some of the best architects within a two-hundred-mile radius and he liked *mine* the best. Mine!

"There is one more thing," I start, knowing the second the truth comes out of my mouth Jenny's going to freak. "I've already met Wyatt Reed before."

"What? Where?"

"At the taco truck."

"Oh no, don't tell me he was the jerk that wouldn't leave you alone?"

I shake my head.

"Oh my gosh." Her eyes widen. "Oh my gosh."

I nod.

"Oh my gosh, I take it back. I'm glad you didn't get his number because this is the best meet-cute of all freaking time!"

"It's not a meet-cute. It was a business meeting with a man I just so happened to have encountered previously. He didn't even recognize me."

"What do you mean?"

"He didn't recognize me. He didn't say anything about that night."

"Well, did you bring it up?"

"No. Why would I?"

"Because maybe he wasn't sure if you wanted to acknowledge what happened. Or maybe he thinks *you* don't remember *him.*"

"I'm pretty sure he didn't recognize me, but it doesn't even matter. This is business and that's where it's staying."

"How boring," Jenny mumbles.

"Oh, whatever. Who cares about a stupid meet-cute. He picked my design! Everything is turning out just perfect."

It isn't until the reality of my situation hits that my heartrate immediately goes back to normal. "I have to tell my dad," I grumble.

Jenny groans. "Seriously? Is that all you think about?"

"What?"

"Your dad doesn't control your life, Luce. Tell him the truth. That this guy saw your design and loved it. That's it."

"It's not that simple."

"Yes, it is. I don't get you sometimes."

"What do you mean?"

"You're so tough when you're out in the world doing your job. You demand respect from people when they won't give it to you, you rarely take no for an answer. You work in construction, Lucy, talk about a man's world. But somehow you always hold your own."

I'd appreciate the compliments if I didn't know there was a giant 'but' coming.

"But..."

There it is.

"Whenever it comes to your dad or the family you just...shut down."

"It's complicated," I argue.

"No, it's not. It's actually really simple. Fight for yourself for once."

"I fight for myself. You just said I never take no for an answer."

"Yeah, about your job. You're fighting for a company, a project, the family business. Gosh, Lucy, you're fighting for your dad. Fight for yourself."

Fight for yourself.

If I could only get Jenny's voice out of my head. I know my dad is going to want to talk about the project to see how the first meeting went and I have no idea what to say. I told him yesterday after I sent the contract that we were a go, but I didn't give him many details after that.

I spent hours last night redrawing my design digitally to send to Foreman so he could start getting supplies ordered. That kept me up until midnight. The hours I laid awake after that were spent rehearsing what I would tell my dad when he asked questions I didn't want to answer.

I'm chewing on the tip of my pen cap as I tend to do when I get nervous. I must be really nervous though because I suddenly have to spit out a giant chunk of plastic.

"Gross, blah," I chuck the pen and suck in a breath when I hear the front door open.

"Morning, Lucy Rae."

Here we go.

"Hey, Dad," I call.

He walks around the corner with a smile. "Tell me about the meeting."

Man, we're not wasting any time here are we?

I grab a new pen and my blue binder and follow him into his office.

"It went great," I smile as I take a seat in the chair across from him as he leans back in his. "The contract is signed. I have Foreman on it already. I called him on my way in this morning. I sent him an email with the details and he's getting everything ordered. We start next Monday. They're gonna tear down the south wall and we're adding a little under a thousand square feet to their floor plan. We should be done with it by mid-November. We're aiming to finish the week before Thanksgiving."

"Sounds like you have everything in order," he smiles.

I nod. "I do. I'm going to go early on Monday to make sure everything's good to go and tie up any loose ends if needed, but so far it's been a very smooth and quick process. We might have to pay a little overtime because the crew will overlap for a week or two with the Johnson project, but that's almost done."

"Do you need help with anything?" he asks.

I shake my head with a grin. "Nope. I got this."

He smiles. "Good. Are you coming to dinner Monday night?"

I pause a moment realizing we're done with the conversation. He asked no questions about the architect or design. Nothing about what kind of renovations we're doing.

It's the first time, in fact, that he hasn't asked for every teeny-tiny unnecessary detail on a project that I'm heading.

Maybe he does trust me after all.

No, that can't be it.

What's his game here?

I tuck my hair behind my ear, waiting for the other shoe to drop. "Yeah, I'll be there."

"Good, your mother will be happy."

My mother acts like I never go home, but I'm the only one that goes to family dinner every Monday. My parents started it a few years ago after we all moved out of the house. My brothers all take turns coming, but I go every week. Luke says I'm being a kiss-up. He's not necessarily wrong, but I prefer to call it being a doting daughter.

"Anything else?" I ask, but he just shakes his head, eyes on his computer.

"Nope, that was it."

"Great, well, I'll just head back to my desk, then."

I scurry out of the office and plop myself in my desk chair unsure what to do next. On one hand I'm relieved because I avoided the exact topic I wanted to avoid. On the other hand, I wonder if my father and I will ever get past the skirting around each other's feelings and start actually communicating.

I could be up front with him. I could tell him the truth. Jenny's right, it's not a big deal to include myself in our list of architects. People don't have to choose my designs.

But I've spent my whole life working toward being a project manager with *Snow Better Builders* and I've yet to make that happen.

Why should architecture be any different?

chapter eleven
wyatt

"Why are you so fidgety?"

I look up from my watch to catch Walker staring at me.

"I'm not fidgety."

"You haven't stopped moving all morning and you keep staring at your watch." He nods toward my wrist.

I drop my left hand in my pocket and run the other down my face.

Okay, maybe I am a little bit fidgety today.

"So, what's the deal?" He raises an eyebrow knowing exactly what the deal is.

Construction starts today.

Everything was finalized within twenty-four hours of our meeting. Lucy was extremely thorough and honest. A little too honest even. She sent me the contract and I signed it and responded within ten minutes. I'd barely put my phone down from sending the email when it began to ring with a number I vaguely recognized.

"You already signed the contract?" she asked when I picked up. No hello or pleasantries. She was right to the point.

"Did you not want me to sign it?" I chuckled.

"No, no," she fumbled. "Of course, I wanted you to sign it. But you never asked any questions about pricing or time-frame expectations. I mean, I sent it to you twenty minutes ago, did you even read it?"

"I...skimmed it," I replied honestly.

"Mr. Reed," she started, but I interrupted her.

"Didn't we already cover this?"

She sighed. "Wyatt, there's a lot of fine print in the contract regarding overtime expectations if the project goes over budget and/or longer than the agreed timeline. Don't you want to go through all those details with your partner?"

"Not really, no," I said. "We covered everything in person."

"We didn't cover *everything*."

"We covered enough."

"I really think – "

I interrupted her again with a chuckle. "I'm starting to think you're trying to change my mind and don't actually want this job."

"No! I'm sorry," she took a deep breath. "Thank you for signing the contract. I'll get everything in order and email you with the details, but we should be ready to start in two weeks. I'll send you an email the Friday before just to make sure we're ready to go Monday morning."

"Sounds great."

We ended the call there and just as she said, she'd emailed me within a few hours with the entire construction schedule and when we would have to close down. She was the most impressive vendor I'd worked with thus far.

And I had to keep reminding myself that her coming today had nothing to do with the fact that I changed my shirt four times this morning before I decided which one looked the best and even put on cologne. It's been so long since I've done that, I had to dig the cologne out of the back of my bathroom cupboard and scrape the crusty parts off the nozzle to make it work.

Her confirmation email came through last Friday as promised, letting us know the crew would be in at 7am and she'd like us here to sign a few waivers.

It's only six-fifteen. Well, six-seventeen and twenty-two seconds to be exact. Not that I've been looking at my watch that much.

I shrug, trying my best at nonchalance, but I don't think I'm selling it. "I'm just eager to get started on the expansion."

"Oh, yeah," he grins. "I wonder why that is."

"It has nothing to do with anything other than I'd like it to be done so we can start taking in bigger crowds and make more money," I argue.

"Right," he feigns a stern look, "it's all about the money." He looks over my shoulder and smirks. "It has absolutely nothing to do with a petite blonde that's here forty-five minutes early."

I turn my head so fast I'm surprised I don't get whiplash.

There she is, peeking into the front door.

"Wyatt?" she calls, knocking on the front door.

I hurry to let her in, absently running my hand through my messy hair. I'm faintly aware of Walker following behind me. I'm almost to the door when I hear him mumble, "All about the money my ass."

I choose to ignore him and open the door.

She's standing tall, smiling bright and excited, blue binder in hand.

"Good morning," she says.

I smile. "Morning."

She seems smaller today. I take her in from head to toe and find her in jeans and work boots. She's not wearing heels. The top of her head just reaches my shoulders, but she exudes enough confidence to feel like she's towering over me.

"I know I'm a little early," she says, brushing past me into the dining room and I hold my breath to avoid the faint smell of fruit, but it hits me anyway. I don't even have time to invite her in. She invited herself.

"I just wanted to go over a few things to make sure we're ready for when the team gets here. I tried to call, but my phone wouldn't dial out for some reason."

"That's okay." I motion toward Walker. "This is my brother and business partner, Walker Reed."

"Ah," she says, extending her hand. "The other Mr. Reed."

He chuckles as he shakes her hand quickly. "Walker is just fine."

She smiles and turns back to me. "Should we sit? I just wanted to go over with you what areas will need to be closed down and when. I know I sent you a copy, but I technically have to get a signature that you understand the areas you shouldn't go during construction. I'll also need any of your staff that might be working during construction to sign waivers. Safety and all that. We have a pretty good schedule from the foreman, and he thinks you'll only have to close fully for the first four weeks while we teardown and then rebuild the south wall. Otherwise, you can probably stay open at half capacity so long as we have everything enclosed while we finish the inside."

"That's great," Walker says pulling out a chair, but she's already moving. She's always moving it seems. Never slowing down.

"We'll put a temporary wall right here," she begins as she walks toward the southern part of the room. "It will be floor to ceiling and we'll have door so you can get through if necessary, but only the foreman and myself will have a key.

For safety reasons, we can't even provide you two with a key."

"No worries, that will be fine."

"It's pretty convenient that you guys are only open for dinner," she continues with a grin. "That way we're not on much of a daily time crunch. The guys can work a full day and only have to start two hours earlier than normal in order to be done before you open for customers. Today I have them coming in at seven, but they'll be here at five starting tomorrow and the rest of the construction. They're actually pretty excited about getting home early, so it works for everyone!"

She's talking a million miles a minute and I have to concentrate to catch each word, but I find myself eagerly waiting to hear what else she has to say. I've never been so interested in construction.

"Anyhoo, how do you feel about porta potties? That's one thing I forgot to go over with you. Since the bathroom will be closed off the whole time, we need a backup plan. You're gonna need some urinals, if you know what I mean," she gives me a look out of the corner of her eye before she goes on, making me chuckle. "You can always go with the traditional blue that looks like you'd rather gauge your eyes out with a crochet hook than step foot into one and risk all kinds of infection, but there are some nicer options available. Like, trailers that get towed in. It's a bit more expensive, but with the atmosphere you guys have going on here, I really think it would be the best option."

She looks between me and Walker.

"But of course, that's up to you guys, just know it's an option."

I turn toward Walker whose eyes are wide as saucers. Probably trying to keep up with all she just said in such a short amount of time.

"Sorry, I tend to talk fast when I get excited. Do I need to go over any of that again?"

"No need to apologize," I say. "I got it all. Sounds like we picked the right girl."

She blushes softly but turns her head away trying to hide it. I hear Walker cough behind me.

"The crew should be here shortly," she continues. "You guys are more than welcome to stay, but it's gonna be limited space for a while. As discussed, we will make sure the back door and office are always accessible. Also convenient that it's on the opposite side of the expansion. Is there anything you guys need from me before we start closing things off?"

I could think of a few things I need. Most of which are highly inappropriate and not at all what she's offering.

"Sounds like you have it under control," I say a bit too loudly, trying to clear my head. "We've posted everywhere that we'll be closed for a few weeks, but we're expecting some foot traffic. Are we able to block off the parking lot?"

"Yes," she smiles. "That's the first order of business. We'll block off the majority of the parking lot at first. I told all my guys they had to park in the lot next door and we'll put the site trailer there as well. We also have a sign that we usually put on the street that says under construction with our logo. It works as a 'closed' sign as well as advertisement for us."

"Great," I smile.

She grins back and I'm not sure how long we stare at each other before Walker clears his throat breaking our contact.

"Well, with the dining room closed for the next four weeks, you probably won't see me much, except for the two catering jobs next week. The kitchen will be accessible throughout all the construction, right?"

"Yes," Lucy nods.

He pats me on the back. "Great. Wyatt will be here most days working in the office if you need anything. I have to head out, but it was great to meet you."

"You too, thank you," she smiles.

"Text me if you need anything," he says to me before leaving through the back door.

She looks at me with a grin and stands straighter. "So, about those porta potties."

chapter twelve
lucy

I've caught him watching me multiple times today. And I'd probably be irritated if I wasn't also seeking him out. I only know he's been watching me because my eyes have been in a constant swivel all day looking for his.

It's ridiculous. And utterly unprofessional. It has me so flustered I'm saying things like 'utterly.'

I don't get this flustered over men. Ever.

I had a boyfriend my senior year of high school. My one and only long-term boyfriend I'm afraid to admit. Matty Williams who was tall, dark and handsome. Much like someone else across the room. He was on the basketball team and had beautiful hair. As much as I hate to admit it now, that hair was ninety percent of the reason I dated him. We looked good together, but it probably comes as no surprise that it didn't last very long. Not after I found him making out with Trisha Holland on the football field after the Sadie Hawkins Dance the January before we graduated. He didn't even play football.

We'd planned to go to school together at NYU, but clearly he had better things to do. Like Trisha Holland.

Jenny and I may or may not have toilet papered his house later that day. Which wasn't that big of a deal until it started raining.

Oh, well. Matthew Bartholomew Williams went on to an Ivy League school and just became the tenth draft pick for the NBA. I don't think he cares too much about the wet toilet paper that's probably still stuck in the maple tree in his parents front yard. My fault for ever dating a guy with the middle name Bartholomew.

It taught me a valuable lesson though, don't waste your time on pretty boys. You know, the boys with sharp jaw lines and flowy hair they pretend is natural, but you know for a fact they spend more time blow drying it than you do yours? Those kinds of boys.

Wyatt Reed is a pretty boy. Though, I'd argue his hair is, in fact, naturally flowy.

How irritating.

College was a bit better on the dating front, but not by much. Most of it was flings except my sophomore year when things got a little serious with Jacob Kent. But I'm sure I don't have to say that things didn't end well with Jake. Things rarely end well with guys named Jake.

When I got here Monday, he hung around for maybe an hour before he left us to our business. It's been five days of construction and I haven't seen him once. It's not uncommon. Most people don't hang around a construction site. Every once and a while we get someone who wants to micromanage our projects and sticks around the whole time telling us how we should be doing our job. Those people irritate me. We know how to do our job, leave us alone. This time, though, I find myself feeling slightly disappointed he hasn't been around.

"Looking for something?"

The deep voice startles me out of my thoughts, and I look up to find the aforementioned pretty boy standing in front me. His hair falling perfectly onto his forehead. So perfectly, he has to run his hands through it to brush it away like a freaking shampoo commercial.

Yeah, that's definitely natural.

"What?" I ask, not sure what he means.

"You've been looking off into space for the last five minutes. I thought you were staring at me, but I don't think you'd flatter me that way," he grins as he rests his hip against my work table.

"You guess correctly."

He chuckles and motions toward the work in front of me. "What are you doing?"

I smile, turning back toward the table. Work I can easily talk about. "Sanding."

He raises an eyebrow. "Why?"

I look at him in confusion. He may be a pretty boy, but he doesn't strike me as the kind of person who doesn't know the basics of building. "Wood gets rough when it's cut, even if it was already sanded – "

His chuckle cuts me off. "I know that part. I meant why are *you* sanding it?"

"Oh," I shrug. "For fun."

Both eyebrows go up this time. "You're sanding for fun?"

I nod. "We'll need it next week. Demolition should be finished today and I want to get a head start before the weekend."

"Is that common for contractors?"

"Finding sanding fun? Yes," I smile. "It's a requirement even. They make you take a polygraph and everything."

He smiles fully, showing off his teeth as he shoves his hands in his pockets. Good lord, why must he be so flawless? Real men don't look like this.

"Well, I don't see anyone else lining up for the sanding table, guess that's why you're the manager," he smirks.

He's flirting with me. And I should tell him to stop.

I really, really should.

"You'd guess right again," I smile. I guess that's a no on the telling him to stop then.

"How long have you been a contractor?"

"Still trying to figure out my age, Mr. Reed?"

"Of course not, Miss Snow, I believe I was informed it was irrelevant." Does he ever stop smiling? "Just making conversation."

I smile in return because how can I not when he offers me the most perfect crooked grin of all time putting every single one of Jenny's book boyfriends to shame. "Well, project manager would be the correct term." I start as I sort out my pieces in order from largest to smallest. I always like to start with the harder pieces first. "I've worked for my dad's company since I was fifteen. He's the general contractor, I just work under his license. Started as a receptionist and just sort of..." I trail off, not sure how to move forward considering I'm not *technically* a manager yet. But semantics. "Evolved."

"And when did you decide you wanted to be an architect?"

My eyes shoot up to his, work forgotten. "Excuse me?"

"The design I picked; it was yours, wasn't it?"

"How did you know?" I ask timidly.

"Well, the note you so subtly snatched off the back was the first clue," he chuckles. "The second was the look on your face when I picked it."

"Is that why you picked it? Because it was mine?" I question, feeling suddenly deflated. Did he pick he because he felt like he had to? Like if he didn't pick mine I wouldn't do a good job on the renovations?

He shakes his head. "No. I picked it because it was the best option. Just a happy coincidence that it was yours."

I'm not completely convinced. "I'm not experienced, Mr. Reed. I've never designed something that actually came to life before."

"I'd have to disagree with that," he says.

My eyebrows bunch. "What do you mean?"

"Your design came to life on the page, Lucy. That's why I picked it."

He doesn't give me a chance to respond. He turns sharply, leaving me at my sanding table with my mouth hanging open.

"I'm thinking peanut butter with raspberries and sardines."

"I'm thinking you're insane," I say with a mouthful of ice cream.

"Come on, Janice wouldn't even know. Her taste buds have completely disintegrated at this point," Jenny says. "We could throw whatever we wanted into a pie and she'd still eat it. She's turning like a hundred."

"Eighty-two."

"Do we really have to get her something? I mean, did we get her something for her birthday last year?"

"I don't remember." I mumble as I take in all the pie options in the display case in front of me. "Oh, didn't she go to California to visit Uncle Jed."

"Yeah, she should've stayed there."

"She's not that bad," I argue.

Her head lulls to the side to glare at me out of the corner of her eye. "She told me last week I had child-bearing hips and I could easily carry twins or triplets."

I hide my laugh behind my ice cream cup and Jenny rolls her eyes.

"Let's just do a raspberry," I decide. "It's a classic. And it's on discount this week. We can have it delivered to her."

I give the checkout girl my credit card and the address for delivery and we leave the bakery with our ice cream in hand as we walk down main street.

"Enough about Janice, did you ever talk to your boss about the new guy at work?"

She throws her head back with a groan. "No. I found out he's the bosses nephew! Can you believe that? Total nepotism."

Jenny's been on the verge of a breakdown over a new hire at work. Jenny's the director of Human Resources and reports to the CFO. The CFO who recently retired.

"Carol was just the greatest, you know. Especially in that role! Women are never CFO's, it was refreshing. And then she leaves and they bring in Dr. Wannabe McDreamy who waltzes in and changes everything. We were doing just fine."

From what I hear, he's a few months younger than Jenny and doesn't have much experience under his belt, but sometimes you have to take what Jenny says with a grain of salt. She tends to be melodramatic.

"What is he changing?"

"Everything! He doesn't like that I organize my files by first name when he thinks it should be by last name." She takes a big bite of ice cream and sighs. "I mean, does he really have nothing better to do than nitpick how I sort *my* files?"

"Sounds like he has a crush on you."

She scoffs. "That's the most absurd thing I've ever heard in my entire existence."

"I doubt that."

"What about you? Did your dad say anything about the design?"

"Actually," I smirk. "He never asked."

"And you didn't tell him about it?" She scrunches her eyebrows.

I shake my head and her mouth drops open as she stops in the middle of the sidewalk. Ice cream slowly falling down her chin.

"Shut your mouth, you look disgusting."

"Excuse me? Perfect little Lucy Rae *lied* to her father?"

"I did not lie."

"It's a lie by omission."

"Semantics."

"I'm so proud of you. My little Lucy Rae is finally growing up."

"It's not a good thing, Jenny. I shouldn't lie to my dad."

"So, it is a lie?"

"Shut up," I stand, throwing my empty bowl in the trash. "Let's go."

"Okay, but for real, I will never understand your relationship with your dad. You two have horrible communication skills."

"We do not."

She simply raises her eyebrows.

"Only about business," I concede.

"Your entire relationship is the business."

"Let's just go please," I stand by her car, waiting for her to unlock it.

"Fine," she unlocks the car. "I just can't wait until you really start to break the rules and I find out you snuck that sexy Wyatt Reed into the janitors closet."

I give her a light shove on the arm as we slide into the car and I do everything I can not to picture myself pressed up against Wyatt Reed in a janitor's closet.

I'm unsuccessful.

chapter thirteen
wyatt

Two weeks. She's been in my restaurant for ten whole business days and I haven't done or said anything that wasn't completely professional. Take that, Walker!

Well, unless you count our conversation about her design. But that wasn't entirely unprofessional. Just playing on the line a bit.

I avoided the restaurant like the plague the first four days, but work has to get done. I had purchase orders to process and vendors waiting for answers. I had to go into the office on Friday.

And there she was with safety glasses and work boots at a sanding bench. Sanding. Not a sight I expected to see.

And one I enjoyed far too much.

Honestly, I haven't had much of an opportunity to say anything unprofessional considering I didn't come in last week and may or may not have snuck in the back when no one was looking today. I've been hiding in the office for the last twenty minutes reminding myself I'm a grown man who doesn't need to hide from a tiny little woman, but I'm pretty sure she could take me down in a second.

I'm not proud of it, but what else am I supposed to do? Talk to her? That's far too risky.

Sneaking around them was easy, considering it's such a small crew. Smaller than I expected. Besides Lucy, and the foreman named Foreman that had Walker laughing for hours, there's only six other men here.

I was worried it would be packed with people and I wouldn't be able to get any work done while they were here, but luckily it's been fairly quiet. Except the occasional power tool or staple gun.

Some of the work I could do at home, but I find bringing work home can be exhausting and if I'm being honest, I'm doing everything I can to stay busy enough to stop thinking about a certain someone who is pregnant and all the things that bit of information brings back up.

I'm just shutting off my computer a little after lunch, ready to sneak out of here when there's a soft knock on the door.

I look up to find said siren in my office doorway.

"Sorry to bother you," she starts with a shy smile. She's wearing her work boots again today, with muddy jeans. Her hair is in two little pigtails sticking out below her hard hat and her eyes are wide behind her safety glasses. Her shirt, that I believe used to be white, is covered in dirt and mud and a few questionable colors I'd rather not know the source of. She looks like she's been doing all the grunt work.

Is that even her job? Shouldn't the other six men be doing the hard labor?

I remind myself this is none of my business and I shouldn't care what kind of work she's doing before I reply, "Not a bother. What's up?"

"Well," she takes a small step into the office, careful not to get too close to the rug. "Foreman's been trying to shut off the water and we're having some issues. There's a valve I found in the back, but it's only shutting off the kitchen water. I called the city and, well, they weren't much help. Do you know where we can shut off the water?"

"Yeah, it's next door." I stand, grabbing my key off the desk. "Follow me." I motion and she trails behind me as I exit through the backdoor of the office. "The two lots share some water lines. It's messy, the city only has half the plans. Honestly, I couldn't even tell you why it is the way it is, we've just delt with it over the years."

We make it across the street and I bend down until I'm eye level with the valve that's tucked behind a maple tree and way too close to the building. "It's just right here, can you see it? It's really hard to get to. Again, I have no idea why any of the water is the way it is. It's a wreck."

"Oh, I can get to that. This would be where my small stature comes in handy," she smiles before shimmying herself behind the tree that's so close to the building, she barely fits. But she manages and turns the pipe with a small grunt. "Got it!"

She scurries back around the tree to smile up at me. "Thanks for that. Do you have the diagrams of the pipes by chance? That way, we don't have to bother you again."

"It's not a bother, really. If you need anything just ask."

She raises a skeptical eyebrow. "You sure? Cause it kind of seemed like you were trying not to be seen."

"What do you mean?"

"I mean, the parking across the street and the sneaking in the back when you thought no one is looking," she says with a small smirk.

Guess I wasn't so sneaky after all.

"Uh, yeah, I just didn't want to get in the way."

"It's your property. If anything, we're going to get in *your* way."

"Maybe we can both agree neither of us is in each other's way."

She giggles and sticks her hand out for a handshake. "Sounds like a plan."

I chuckle as I place my hand in hers and shake it once. "Sounds good."

"Thanks again for the help," she smiles, slipping her hand from mine. "Will you be here long? The crew was going to get some lunch around eleven, we can bring something back for you?"

"That's okay, I'll probably grab some tacos or something on my way home."

Her eyes light up just a bit at the mention of tacos and she lifts up on her toes a little when she says, "Where do you usually get tacos?"

She shoves her glasses up her nose as if she's uncomfortable with the question and for the first time since we officially met, I wonder if she does actually remember our first meeting.

"The taco truck in the grocery store parking lot on main."

"I love that place!" she squeals. "My cousin Jenny and I go there all the time. What's your go-to order?"

"Four steak tacos with guacamole. If you don't get their guac what's the point?"

"I know! My order is – "

"Two grilled chicken tacos with guacamole."

Her eyes bug out of her head and a million emotions cross her face before her grin widens.

"So you do remember me?"

How could I have forgotten?

"I don't really make a habit of rescuing desperate women from crazed men, so yeah I remember."

"Okay, desperate is a bit of an exaggeration, I was handling myself just fine."

"I'm sure you were. Just figured a little help wouldn't hurt."

She giggles. "It didn't hurt. Why didn't you say anything?"

I shrug. "You didn't say anything, either. I figured you didn't remember me."

"Definitely remembered you," she mumbles.

We stand there for a beat, our eyes glued to each other when I finally clear my throat.

"Well, let me know if you need anything."

"I will! I'll, uh, I'll see you around?" she says, walking backward toward the restaurant.

"Yeah, I'll see you around. All of the floor plans and everything are on the bookshelf in my office. You're welcome to grab anything you need, whenever you need it."

"Thanks, Wyatt," she smiles once more before turning on her heel and marching back to the restaurant. She stuffs her safety glasses in her back pocket, bringing my attention to the last place it should be. I roll my eyes and sigh at myself before I make the trek across the parking lot. I keep my gaze on the ground until I reach the back door and look up just long enough to see her head already turned toward me.

"Just one more, pleeeease!" his small voice carries in the chocolate shop and he drags out the 'please' so long the old lady behind us glares.

"Lincoln, I've already given you way too much. Your mom's gonna have a cow when we get home."

"We're getting a cow?" his eyes shimmer.

"No," I chuckle. "It's just a figure of speech."

His face contorts into confusion. "What's a figure of speech?"

I picked Lincoln up on my way home from the restaurant and took him for pizza, arcade games and ice cream. It's our usual Friday night. Walker and Dannie go on a date night before the restaurant opens for a late lunch and I take Lincoln for the afternoon. But we drove past this new chocolate shop in town and he begged me for a piece. I agreed to one little piece on the way home. Thirty minutes and seven chocolates later, we're still here.

"A figure of speech is just an expression."

His small face contorts even more. "What's an expression?"

This is what no one prepares you for with kids – that they never stop asking questions.

"I don't know, ask your mom," I reply, handing him the box of remaining chocolate. I'm weak when it comes to him, even though I know Ellie's wrath will be waiting for me when I drop him off with a sugar rush. If he asked me for the moon, I'd figure out a way to get it for him. I just can't say no.

"Mom's really smart. She knows everything."

I smile. "Yeah, your mom is really smart."

He pops another chocolate into his mouth, that's eight. Ellie's gonna kill me. "Mom says that she's so smart because she went to school."

"Well, school does make you smarter."

"I don't like school."

My eyebrows come together. "Since when? I thought you loved school."

"Not anymore!" he shakes his head from side to side.

"Why not?"

"Because Missy gave Carter her snack pack."

I have no idea who Missy or Carter is, so I ask, "Why does that make you not like school?"

He looks up at me, chocolate all over his face. "Because she used to give *me* her snack packs and now she gives them to Carter."

Ah, the drama of a kindergarten class. I nudge his shoulder. "Do you like Missy?"

"I did, but not anymore! Mom says I'm too little for a girlfriend."

I do my best to stifle my laugh. "Was Missy your girlfriend?"

He gives me the most impatient look like I'm the dumbest person in the world. "Duh, she gave me her snack pack."

"Right. But now she's Carter's girlfriend because she shared her snack pack with him?"

He nods once, popping yet another chocolate into his mouth. Nine and counting..

"Well, I think your mom is right. You're too little to have a girlfriend."

"Wyatt, I'm five. I'm not little anymore."

"Well, you're littler than me."

"Yeah, but when I grow up, I'll be as big as you. That's what mom says."

"Your dad is tall, too."

"Not as tall as you!"

"Yeah," I mumble trying not to think about all the ways he's like me.

He shoves the last chocolate in his mouth and asks, "Do you have a girlfriend?"

I shake my head. "Nope."

"Did you used to have a girlfriend?"

He's licking the chocolate off his fingers and his eyes are wide – completely oblivious to how hard that question is to hear. How hard it shouldn't be to answer.

"Yeah, buddy, I used to."

"How come you don't anymore?"

He's so young, his questions are simple. He knows nothing of the weight I carry, the guilt I feel for how things are. How confusing it is to feel that regret while also being happy with the life that he has. So many thoughts fill my mind, but for now I just reply, "I stopped sharing my snack packs with her."

"That's not very nice of you."

I shake my head. "No, it wasn't very nice of me. But she's really happy now. She has a new boyfriend and they love each other."

"Did you love her?"

I nod, trying to ignore the knot forming in my stomach.

"Did you love her like Daddy loves Mommy?"

I smile, grateful he has parents as strong as he does. That even at five years old he can see how much they love each other.

"No, buddy, I didn't love her like Daddy."

chapter fourteen
lucy

"I need to understand what, exactly, Ricky Ricardo's show at the *Tropicana* was. Does anyone actually know? Every episode is so random."

It's nine on a Friday night and Jenny's already two popcorn bags deep. I can't count how many sour gummies I've eaten in the last twenty minutes. My stomach feels like it's about to explode and still I reach for the popcorn bowl in her lap.

"Don't diss Lucy."

"I'm not. I'm dissing Ricky," Jenny argues. "Let her in the show, for pete's sake, it'd be more interesting."

She's not wrong, but I refuse to let anyone diss on the greatest show of all time.

"*I Love Lucy* is a classic. It's timeless. We just let the plot holes go."

I could watch this show muted, without subtitles and still be able to quote every word of every episode. I've loved it since I was a kid. My parents claim they got my name from a book my mom read when she was a teenager, but I claim Miss Ball as the inspiration.

"Fine."

"Any update on Mr. Wannabe McDreamy?"

"Oh, please, we are not calling him that."

"I don't know his name."

"Because I refuse to waste the energy it requires to say it on him."

"You're the most dramatic person I know."

"I know, isn't it wonderful?" She tosses her hair. "What about you? How's everything going with the new test project?"

"Really good actually. It's only been two weeks, but the teardown on the south wall went so smooth I couldn't even believe it. And then we – "

She scoffs, interrupting me. "You know I'm not talking about the actual project. Construction, blah!"

I roll my eyes and steal the popcorn. "We're not talking about anything except construction."

"You're the most boring person I know." She rolls her eyes, taking the popcorn back.

I chuckle. This is why we work.

"What about your dad, or is that topic off limits too?"

"Honestly, I haven't seen him much. Him and my mom have been gone all week at their timeshare in New Hampshire. He'll be back on Monday, though."

He gave me a passing kiss on the cheek as I he left for the day on Tuesday. Along with a stack of invoices he'd been hoarding at his desk that I ended up having to stay late to pay.

"Perfect time to break some rules."

"And what rules should I be breaking exactly?"

"All of them."

"Some of us like the rules."

"Yeah, boring people."

"Why am I friends with you again?"

"Because even though I should keep my mouth shut most of the time – "

"More like all of the time," I mumble, but she ignore me.

"You still love me. Seriously, though, he doesn't know you're using your design?"

"No, and I still feel guilty about that. Honestly, I don't even know why I kept it a secret. It's not like he'd get mad at me or anything."

In my twenty-five years of life, my father has never yelled at me. I don't even remember ever getting in trouble when I was little. Because I was perfect Little Lucy Rae since I came out of the womb.

But there was something about letting everyone know it was my design that we were constructing. It left a pit in my stomach that felt a lot like fear, but I don't like using that kind of language.

"It's because y'all have horrible communication skills."

"We're back to that?"

"Because it's true. Has your dad ever actually told you why he won't make you a manager? No. Have you ever told your dad exactly how important this is to you and why you want to be a part of the family business so bad? No. You don't get what you don't ask for. Until you two start being honest with each other you're going to die still stuck in this cycle."

"I hate when you're right."

"Which is always. I don't know why you even argue, anymore." She props one hand under her head and smirks. "Now, about that Wyatt Reed."

"We're definitely not going there."

"But you want to?"

"I didn't say that."

"But you didn't not say it either."

"That sentence makes no sense." I grab another piece of candy, as my stomach continues to protest. "What's your obsession with him anyway? You haven't even seen him."

"I'm not obsessed with him, but it's obvious you like him."

I laugh once, sitting up straighter as I turn the volume down on the TV. "Jenny, I've talked to him all of, like, five times. He's a client. Nothing more, nothing less."

When I got home from the restaurant, I felt it necessary to keep the little bit of information that Wyatt did actually remember me from Jenny. She would make a mountain out of a mole hill and I didn't need that right now.

I have my own feeling about Wyatt to work through, I don't need Jenny's in the mix, too.

"I know you better than anyone. Just admit you like him."

I groan as she moves and sits next to me on the couch. "I might, maybe, just a little-tiny-itty-bitty-bit find him *slightly* attractive."

"I knew it!" she yelps and I cover my ears. "You're in love!"

"How in the world," I yell over her excitement, "did you get love from 'maybe just a little-tiny-itty-bitty-bit?'"

"It's all about what's left unsaid. You need to read between the lines."

She takes the remote from me and turns the volume back up. "And before you tell me that it would be unprofessional and your dad wouldn't approve, think about yourself and what you want."

"But it *would* be unprofessional. And my dad *wouldn't* approve."

"So?"

"What do you mean, so?" I practically yell. "It's business. You work in HR, you know better than anyone not to mix business with pleasure."

"Oh, please, I made out with a new guy in finance last week."

That has me pausing for a beat. "Okay, I'm going to need more details on that one."

She waves her hand at me dismissively. "Oh, it was nothing. We both worked late, had too many lemon bars and ended up making out in the janitor's closet."

"What's with you and janitor's closets?"

"It's dark, quiet and small," she looks at me out of the corner of her eye. "You should really try it sometime."

"If you say the words Wyatt or Reed, I'm going to smack you. Give me the popcorn and lets just watch the show."

"Fine, but when you do finally crack and end up in the janitor's closet, give me a heads up. I'll clear my schedule for the deets."

Saturdays are my least favorite day.

I know, I'm insane.

There's just way too many people on the road, everyone out shopping, partying and who knows what else. The stores are all jampacked. And worse, there's no schedule or structure. It's just twenty-four hours where people willy-nilly about all day, with no idea where they're going or how long they'll stay there.

It's horrible.

I, however, have my schedule to stick to. Even on Saturdays. It's my run day. I usually run at the park, bright and early with the sun. My brothers think I'm insane for waking up at 5:30am on a Saturday to run, but we all have our ways of relaxation. Running is mine.

It's a perfect September day out, the sun shining, the birds chirping, the wind just right to keep me cool.

One lap around the park is exactly 1.04 miles. I know I sound really cool when I talk about how I run every week, but I barely make it that mile and it's more of a very slow jog.

I turn the corner and see the fire hydrant (my personal mile marker) in the distance. My chest hurts, my legs feel like jelly and I'm reconsidering if this really is my form of relaxation. My breathing become more ragged and I'm about to give up when my foot lines up with the hydrant and I immediately throw my body onto the grass, gasping for breath. I'll run another mile, but I need a minute. And by 'run' I mean slowly speed walk.

I close my eyes and take a few deep breaths, trying to bring my heart rate down a bit when I hear a small voice above me.

"Are you dead?"

My eyes pop open to find a small brown-haired boy, maybe five or six, standing over me. He's holding a soccer ball in his small hands and his eyebrows are furrowed.

"Not yet," I pant, "but it feels like I might."

"I saw you fall over and I thought you died."

"Well," I sit up, making me almost reach his small height. "No dead runners here, but I hear there are some dead ducks by the lake."

His eyes widen and a huge grin spreads across his face. I don't know what it is with kids and dead animals, but they're all obsessed. My nieces and nephews never fail to tell me about the dead mice in their garages, the dead birds they find at the park or the dead fish in the lakes. It's kind of creepy, but it's an easy way to connect with them.

"But, uh," I start looking around the park, trying to find an adult who must be tied to him. He can't be here alone. "Are your parents here?"

He shakes his head.

That has my heart rate speeding up again. "Are you here alone?"

He shakes his head again.

"Who are you here with?"

His little mouth opens to respond, but a voice behind me interrupts him. "Lincoln! What are you doing? You can't run that far away from me!"

"I saw this lady fall over and I thought she was dead."

I turn slowly, knowing the face that will appear, that voice somehow already recognizable. I have a quip on the tip of my tongue about not being a dead woman, but all words leave my brain when I turn and catch those chocolate eyes.

"Lucy?"

Wyatt stands straighter, the sun shining just right on his obnoxiously perfect hair. I'm already short, but sitting on the ground, looking up at him makes him seem like a giant and I don't know how I feel about that disadvantage.

I stand up quickly, too quickly. I stumble slightly as stars appear in my vision. Maybe I overdid it on the run. Wyatt's hand gently wraps around my arm to steady me and there goes my heart rate again.

"You okay?" he asks, tightening his hold.

"Yeah," I say, my shallow breathing having absolutely nothing to do with my wannabe run.

He looks at me intently.

"I promise, I'm fine," I assure him. I pull my arm gently from his grasp, but I can still feel the warmth of his fingers. "I'm guessing this little guy belongs to you?"

We both look down at Lincoln who has a huge smile on his face.

"Yeah, sorry if he was bothering you." Wyatt looks down and gives Lincoln a stern look, but it morphs into a smile quickly when Lincoln smiles wide.

The little boy ignores the remark. "The dead lady says there are dead ducks in the lake."

"Her name is Miss Snow and we can go see the dead ducks before we leave."

"Yay!" he jumps up and down in excitement. "Miss Snow, do you want to come see the dead ducks with us?"

"You can call me Lucy," I say to him before turning to Wyatt. "And he wasn't a bother at all. Kind of sweet, actually, that he checked on me when he thought I was dead," I chuckle.

He smiles wider, showing his exceptionally white teeth. "So, he gets to call you Lucy, just like that? I had to work for that privilege."

"He's, like, six, he gets a cute pass."

"I'm five," the little guy says, holding up four fingers.

We both laugh again as Wyatt reaches down and lifts up another one of his fingers.

"Well," I rub my hands on my thighs, why are they so clammy? "Tell his mother that I'm sorry if I traumatized him thinking he found a dead person."

He chuckles quietly, "I think he was more excited at the idea of finding a dead woman than traumatized."

"Right. Maybe you'll want to address that with her too."

"Probably." Does he ever stop smiling?

I pause for a small beat, wondering if he and the mother are together, before berating myself for even questioning. It's not like it matters what a clients' personal life looks like.

"His dad will probably get a kick out of it, it's fine," he adds as almost as an after-thought and an answer to my unasked question.

Client, client, client.

"Wyatt's my uncle!" Lincoln pipes.

Wyatt pats the back of Lincoln's head. "Yeah, the best uncle in the world, right?"

Lincoln thinks for a minute. "Yeah, but only because you buy me chocolate and Brian doesn't."

I smile at the exchange between these two. The genuine smile on Wyatt's face as Lincoln speaks. My heart expanding at the tenderness of their dialogue..

"Well, I should really get going. I have a little bit of work to do today to catch up for Monday. We have the porta potties coming on Monday morning."

"Oh, right," he nods with a grin. "The urinals."

"Yes, the urinals."

"You know, I've got to say, in all my life I've never heard that word as much as I have since you showed up."

"Well, clearly you need learn the art of scintillating conversation."

He laughs again, a bit more confident this time and forget my heart racing; I think it just completely stopped.

I push my glasses up the bridge of my nose just for something to do with my hands as I take a few backward steps toward my car.

"Well, anyway, I'll see you Monday."

"Have a good weekend, Lucy." Wyatt smiles before taking Lincoln's hand and leading him toward the lake, lifting the small child easily with one hand each time he jumps. Lincoln's little giggle carries all the way to my car.

If Wyatt, with his perfectly chocolate hair and dark eyes and gruff laugh wasn't smoking hot enough, the doting uncle who takes his nephew to the park early on Saturday mornings could light a house on fire.

Heaven help me.

chapter fifteen
wyatt

I still sneak into the office.

I planned to be strong, but one look at Lucy on Monday morning in her combat boots had me suddenly needing to check my empty email box on my phone, until she turned the corner and went inside.

Pretty sure if there was a picture next to the word 'pathetic' in the dictionary, it would be of me sitting in my car hiding from a woman half my size.

There wasn't much work to be done and I honestly, could have done it at home, but I hate working at home. It's one of the best pieces of advice I received from Walker when we started the restaurant.

"Don't take work home, man. Leave it at work. Even if you love your job, leave it at home. The last thing you want is for it to become your whole life, good or bad."

At the time I didn't really understand what he meant, but I think I do now. I love my job. I love working with my family, I love the hours. I love the pay. It's great. Too great. In the last year, I've done exactly what he told me *not* to do. I've let my job become my whole life. I don't have hobbies, I don't do anything for fun. I go to work and then go home and think about work. I go to sleep, dream about work, then wake up and do it all again the next day.

At first, I thought it was good. For the first time in my life I was putting in effort. I was making a consistent living, helping others, *doing* something. As simple as that is, I'd never really done that before. After college, I couldn't keep a job. I think the longest stint I had was with a buddy of mine for six months before I got fired for drinking on the job. Not one of my finest moments.

I've been working hard not to take work home, but that just means I spend more time at the restaurant. The small apartment just too confining sometimes.

Usually, I avoid my place by spending more time at Walker's place, but that's also been a place of avoidance for me lately. Ellie's started to get irritable and I can't go four seconds without the reminder of all the mistakes I've made.

So the office it is.

I've mostly stayed hidden the last couple days, which I plan to do today. That is until the sound of a staple gun followed by a loud crash and a soft voice saying, "Dagnabbit," has me jumping from my desk before I can think, bolting into the dining room.

"Are you okay?" I ask coming up beside her.

"Oh," she jumps a little, turning toward me. "You startled me. I didn't know you were here." She looks up at me with her big ocean eyes through her safety glasses.

"What happened? Are you okay?" I ask again.

She waves me off, sucking on her thumb. "It's fine. I just stapled my thumb."

My eyes widen and I look at the forgotten staple gun on the floor. "With a staple gun?"

"Yeah," she looks down with me. "I probably broke it. Woops," she giggles around her thumb.

Without thinking, I wrap my fingers around her wrist and pull her thumb from her mouth. Her skin is soft, fingers slender and petite.

Her eyes widen slightly, but she doesn't pull away as I examine her hand. The blood is dripping out quickly and I grab a towel to place under her finger, so nothing drips on the floor.

"Did you pull the staple out?" I marvel.

She nods, still a bit wide-eyed.

"You stapled your hand with a *staple gun* and then pulled it out yourself?" My eyes widen in disbelief.

She nods again.

"And the worst word you said was dagnabbit?"

She shrugs. "It wasn't that bad. I've done it before."

She's so confusing. One second she's waltzing into the restaurant in red heels and the next she's wearing combat boots and pulling staples out of her hand with her perfectly polished nails.

It's like she can read my mind because she says in an impatient tone, "Just because I have blonde hair, painted nails and like to wear heels doesn't mean I don't know how to get my hands dirty."

She pulls her hand from mine and wraps it with some gauze she pulls out of a first aid kit from her bag.

"Touché."

She begins wrapping her thumb carefully and asks, "So where have you been?"

"What do you mean?"

She shrugs. "I haven't seen you all week. Thought maybe you were out of town."

"Oh," I run an awkward hand down my face. "No, I was just...busy." Busy avoiding you.

After running into her at the park on Saturday, I couldn't get her out of my head. Every single time I closed my eyes it was her in the crop top and leggings.

"Oh," she looks back down at her hand and I'm pretty sure I see a blush hit her cheeks. "I thought maybe you were avoiding me, uh, us again."

"No, just...lots going on."

"I guess with the restaurant closed for a couple weeks you guys' kind of get a break, huh?"

"A little bit. Walker more than me."

"Why's that?" she says, wincing slightly as she tightens the wrapping on her finger. The first sign of pain I've seen and if I'd blinked I'd have missed it.

"He's the chef."

"Gotcha. What exactly do you do?"

"Paperwork. I'm technically the accountant, but I also handle all the purchasing and payroll."

"Wow. That sounds like a lot."

I shrug. "It's not bad."

"Are you ready for reopen next week? They should be finishing the insulation today and then drywall wall tomorrow and Friday. I made sure my team understands that starting Monday they have to finish by three everyday so there isn't any overlap with customers."

"Sounds great."

She finishes the wrapping on her thumb and picks up the staple gun. After a quick examination and a test, she continues her work with the unbroken staple gun like she wasn't just dripping blood all over the floor.

"What were you doing, anyway?" I ask.

"Trying to staple the banner to this board so we can post it on the corner." She points to a banner on the floor with their logo. "We had one, but it blew away last night and got run over so I grabbed another one this morning, but it was so tightly wound, I lost my grip trying to hold it straight."

"Do you need help?"

She looks at me a long moment before finally answering. "I can have one of the guys help me."

"You sure? I wouldn't want you to staple your thumb again."

She laughs. "That would happen whether you're here or not, I hate to admit. I have a bad case poor depth perception. But I...uh..." she pushes her safety glasses up her nose, eyeing me up and down. "Yeah, I guess I could use some help. Thank you."

I look around until I find a spare set of safety glasses. I grab them and slide them on my face before catching her eye again. "Lead the way, boss."

She smiles as she holds the staple gun out to me and asks, "Do you know how to get your hands dirty?"

I smirk as I take the staple gun from her hand, my finger brushing her bandaged one. "You have no idea."

chapter sixteen
lucy

Do you know how to get your hands dirty?
You have no idea.

I'd be lying if I said those words haven't been repeating in my head nonstop for the last twenty-four hours. I have no idea what prompted me to ask him that question or even let him help with the work. It's a safety hazard if I've ever seen one. He's not a construction worker, he has no certifications or experience. It took approximately sixty seconds and one 2x4 knocking me in the ribs to know he had no idea what he was doing. Thankfully, the 2x4 was still mostly on the table and it only left a tiny bruise. I didn't know there was a learning curve to a staple gun, but apparently there is. I tried my best not to laugh, worried he would be offended, but he laughed at himself so much I had to join in. After a while we fell into an easy banter as we worked side by side.

"Lucy?"

I'm startled out of my daze.

"You dozed out for a minute," Luke says.

"Sorry, just thinking about work.

"Dad said you had a new project?"

"Yeah, you know that restaurant, *Abe's Place*? They're expanding," I say over a loud rush of yells from the kids.

Today we're celebrating my nephew winning his spelling bee. Our weekly dinners are usually a random mixture of family since not everyone can make it each week, but today everyone is here for the special occasion.

I've been counting down the minutes until tomorrow is over, the stress weighing on me. I keep telling myself I'm stressed because the restaurant is set to reopen on Monday and we still have so much to do, but I'm pretty sure it has a lot more to do with a particular owner who keeps popping up at unexpected times.

"Nice," he replies. "Dad said he gave you full reins."

"He did."

"And did you tell him you've had full reins for the last year?"

I roll my eyes. "No."

He chuckles.

"What am I missing over here, Lucy Rae," Landon asks, plopping down next to me. "I never see you anymore. All you do is work."

"Take it up with my boss," I snap.

"Woah, someone's feisty today," Logan chimes in, taking the empty seat on my other side.

"Maybe I'm feisty because someone's been on paternity leave for almost a year." I glare at Landon.

"Hey, not my fault. Dad told me to take as much time as I want."

"How come he never tells me to take as much time as I want?"

"Because you never ask for it," he argues.

I groan. "That's because the work has to get done. Someone's got to do it."

"I think our little Lucy Rae here needs some T-L-C, don't you think, Logan?" Landon looks over my head to Logan.

"No, guys, don't!" I exclaim, knowing exactly what's coming.

Before I can make a run for it, they trap me between their linked arms and begin to squish me with grins on their faces.

"Come on, Lucy Sandwiches haven't been fun for like a decade. Do boys ever grow up?" I complain, but the laugh comes through without my consent as they squeeze their arms harder.

My brothers are all very close in age. Logan is the oldest at forty, Luke next at thirty-eight and then Landon at thirty-six. Then there's the surprise that is me at twenty-five years young. Having such a big age gap makes our brother/sister relationship unique in many ways. I never shared a house with Logan that I can remember. He left home when I was only five. I remember Luke leaving home, but barely. Landon is the one I remember living with us the most. He stayed home while he went to school and then moved just down the street, spending more time at home than his apartment until he got married two years ago.

"But you're laughing because you secretly love us," Landon says.

"I'm laughing in lieu of knocking your heads off," I grunt through the sandwich. "You're welcome."

Finally, they let me go and I take a deep breath, jumping from the couch. "I'm going outside to have a more civilized conversation with your children."

They all laugh as I turn on my heel and I hear them start talking about the latest basketball game. Men. They're all the same.

"Lucy Rae, can you help me with this?" my mom asks as I walk through the sliding glass door onto the back porch. She has a big box of cookies that she's trying to place neatly on a plate. Carol Snow loves a good presentation. I've never quite understood it. With three boys wreaking havoc all over, it's a miracle our house was always clean, but it was. And as the families grew and grandchildren joined the fun, I figured she would be a little more laid back, but I think it's made her precisions worse. I grab the box from her and hold it while she places the cookies into little heart shapes.

"Your dad said the restaurant project is going well."

I nod. "It's going really well. Everything's been surprisingly smooth so far. No backorders, no one has called in sick yet. We've had full staff with full supplies. It's been great. Knock on wood it stays that way."

"How is everything else going?" she asks with a cheeky grin.

"It's good. Jenny and I are thinking about taking a trip to L.A. for Christmas."

"That would be fun. Your dad and I went to L.A. right before we found out I was pregnant with you."

"I know, I've seen the pictures of dad pretending to throw you in the pacific."

She blushes at the memory and smiles. "It was a wonderful trip."

"Yeah, we're excited."

"Lucy," she asks, eyes on me, her cookies forgotten. "Are you happy?"

The question catches me off guard, the seriousness in her gaze startling. "Of course, I'm happy, why?"

"You just work yourself so hard, I know how much overtime you put in and I worry you don't make enough time for yourself."

I raise a brow. "You mean dating?"

She gives me an impatient look that I know all too well. "No, I mean for *yourself*. If that includes dating, great, but it doesn't have to. I just want to make sure you're doing what *you* want."

I open my mouth to respond and say that I'm doing exactly what I want, but I close it when I feel the uncertainty.

"I guess, I have been feeling a little...stuck lately."

She pats my shoulder with a reassuring smile. "That's very normal. Everyone feels stuck sometimes. Maybe you should talk to your dad."

"Why?"

She laughs once. "I'm not blind, Lucy. I know my children. I know that you're not happy with your position."

I shouldn't feel as shocked as I do by her confession. My mother has always been extremely observant, and we've never been able to hide anything from her. She always knew when one of the boys snuck out or snuck a girl into their room. Whether it was a lie about a grade on a test or skipping school, she always knew. We could never hide anything from her. I shouldn't be surprised that she caught on to this as well.

"Your father is a very stubborn man," she continued, placing her cookies once again, "and very set in his ways. But talk to him. Tell him what you want. I think you'd be surprised."

It's only nine-thirty in the morning and I just want to go home. Three workers called in sick this morning, so I had to rush over to the site to help, even though I'm so behind on invoicing, I'm going to have to stay late at the office tonight to catch up. I spent the entire car ride over to the restaurant calling in backups, only managing to get one who agreed after I offered time and a half for the entire day. I arrived to find a glass window had shattered when the guys were trying to put it in because the sun was glaring off a truck across the street and they couldn't see properly. We turned the water off, or thought we did, to hook up to one of the water lines for the new family restroom, and we flooded half the parking lot because the plans from Wyatt didn't note an extra line that was added later that has its own valve. I've never seen water lines so messy.

This is what I get for saying everything had been perfectly smooth just yesterday. Maybe yesterday is part of the problem. I've been distracted all day, unable to get my conversation with my mom out of my head.

She's right of course, as is Jenny. I need to talk to my dad. But for some reason, I just can't make myself have that conversation.

I managed a little bit of bravery on my way over to the restaurant and stopped at the office, thinking maybe my dad was early. Not that he's ever been early a day in his life and like I don't know his schedule by heart, but unfortunately I missed him.

I slam the door to the trailer right as the clock chimes for one o'clock and drop myself into the cheap desk chair as Foreman's son comes in with a questionable look on his face.

"Jared, if you have bad news for me, just save it for tomorrow. I don't think I can take any more today. This is the Monday-ist Friday of my life." I lean back in the chair and drape my arm over my eyes dramatically.

He chuckles. "Sure thing, boss. I'll just leave these bathroom tiles on the desk here and won't mention they're the wrong color or that they're the wrong size."

"Seriously?" I jump up to examine the tiles and sure thing, they're the wrong size *and* color. "I put that order in myself, I know I ordered it right."

"You did," he says handing me a slip of paper. "I pulled the PO from the system. You ordered right, but these things happen. I'm sure they can overnight the right ones and we'll only be a day or two behind. We aren't scheduled to put the bathroom tile in until next week. We have plenty of time, I promise." He gives me a reassuring pat on the back.

Jared has worked for his dad as long as I've worked for mine. We practically grew up together, though he's a few years older than me. He's a little over thirty, barely taller than me, and knows every single thing a person could possibly know about construction. I'd bet my blue binder he dreams about it. He's been Landon's best friend as long as I can remember. He's practically just another brother considering he spent more time at our house than his own growing up.

"What would I do without you, Jared?"

"You'd survive." He smiles and then leans back to half sit on the desk. "I hate to add fuel to the fire, but we need to get that window ordered or it could delay the restaurant reopen next week. I don't think they will want to have customers eating their food with a gaping hole where a window should be."

I groan. "Don't remind me. I'll talk to Wyatt today and see what they want to do. Unless they want to board it up like an abandoned hotel, we'll probably have to postpone the reopen."

I gather the tiles and pass them back to him. "Can you please call the vendor and have them overnight the correct tiles? Two-day air will suffice, but overnight will make me more inclined to use them again."

He takes the PO back then gives me a salute. "You got it, Boss." He turns sharply on his heel and does a pretend military march to the desk.

I chuckle. "Thanks. You really are a life-saver."

I see a car pull into the parking lot in my peripheral and go around to the back. Wyatt must be here.

I ignore the small jump in my stomach at the thought and clear my throat.

"I'll be back," I say to Jared.

I check myself in the reflection of the trailer door window quickly, tucking my stray hair behind my ears. I've kept my hair short since I started deciding how to style it. My mom cut it for me when I was nine and I never went back. I'm able to put it into two tiny little ponytails while I work, but the front pieces always fall out, no matter what I do.

"You look fine, Lucy. Pretty sure he's already noticed."

I turn quickly and awkwardly smooth my hair down. "I wasn't – "

"Of course, you weren't," he chuckles. "Now go tell the man we got problems. I'm sure he'll understand it much more when it's coming from you."

"It's not like that."

"If you say so."

I drop my hands on my hips. "I didn't realize you were such a gossip."

"I'm not, but I hear things. The whole crew talks about how he's got you flustered."

My mouth drops open. "I am not flustered!"

"I'm just telling you what I heard."

"Well, that's just not true. And you guys shouldn't be gossiping about the – "

I'm interrupted by a knock on the trailer door.

"Speak of the devil," Jared mumbles as Wyatt peeks his head through the window.

I take a deep breath and open the trailer door.

"Good morning, Lucy," Wyatt smiles up at me. It's the first time I haven't had to look up at him and I'm not sure how I feel about it.

Something about the way his eyes peek through his eyelashes as he looks up, half squinting from the sun, has my heart racing and my palms sweating.

I clear my throat. "I was just coming to see you, do you have a minute?"

"I can find a minute for you."

I hear Jared snicker behind me.

"Let's talk down in your office, shall we?" I shoot a side-eyes glare at Jared. "It's a bit crowded in here."

"Yeah, sure."

I grab the doorway to steady myself as I move to take the first step down when his hand shoots out and grabs mine, holding firmly. It gives me pause, this simple chivalrous act of helping a woman down the stairs. I'm wearing jeans and work boots today, not even heels. Of course, I'm perfectly capable of walking down three steps off a small trailer by myself, but it's not about being unable. It's about a man letting a woman know he's there in case she needs him.

Suddenly I feel wobbly on my feet and grip his hand tighter.

"Thank you," I whisper as I take the last step and look up at him.

"Of course." He gestures toward the back door of the restaurant. "After you. We can walk and talk."

"Right, I just wanted to give you a status update," I start as we begin our slow walk. "We've had a few hiccups. Just baby hiccups, nothing crazy, but it might require the restaurant stay closed an extra week."

"What's going on?"

I laugh once. "What's *not* going on. It's been a day. Biggest problem is, we were supposed to get everything closed in today, but two windows got broken and reordering will take at least three days."

"Three days isn't that bad."

"No, but it will push your reopen back another week."

"I mean, isn't the temporary wall there for a reason? Does it really matter if the outer walls are open?"

"The temporary wall isn't insulated or anything. It would be cold and loud from the street. We really need the windows in and everything tightly closed."

He shrugs. "Honestly, I'm not that worried about it. Walker just booked two more catering gigs next week, so we're still doing pretty good. He works too hard anyway. He deserves a bit of a break. We'll probably just stay closed until it's finished. It's only, what, six, seven weeks?"

"Are you sure?"

"Yeah, it's okay. You kind of did us a favor," he nudges my shoulder with his lightly. I stop in my tracks and turn toward him.

His understanding is surprising. I've never told a client we got delayed like this without frustration or accusations thrown my way. Wyatt's looking at me with a faint smile on his face, calm as can be. Thanking me even. Every time I turn around he surprises me.

"Well, thanks for being so understanding. Some people would be yelling at me by now."

He frowns. "Why? It's not your fault."

I shrug. "I mean it is. I'm responsible for the crew, the project. If my crew doesn't do a good job, I don't do a good job. It's my last name on the contract, not theirs."

He looks at me for a long time like he's searching for some kind of answer when he suddenly asks, "How old are you?"

I can't help but smile. "I thought we determined my age was irrelevant?"

"To the job, yes. To this conversation, not so sure. You just...seem very wise, but also very young," his eyebrows come together as he scrutinizes me. "It's confusing sometimes."

I raise a brow. "Are you saying I'm smarter than I look?"

"Yeah."

"So, I look dumb?"

He runs a hand down his face and drops his head down, looking up at me through those darn eyelashes again. "Not what I meant."

"It's okay," I pretend to toss my hair over my shoulder. "The blonde hair's just a disguise. I actually have an IQ of two-hundred-and-one."

He looks back at me with a relaxed grin on his face that could take a girl's breath away, but not this one. Because she's a professional.

"In all seriousness, though," I speak slowly, gauging his reaction. "I'm twenty-five."

I'm very young for what I do, that's not a secret, and I do have a baby face. Most people assume I'm barely legal. In his defense, though, he doesn't look surprised or shocked. Honestly, he doesn't give me much of a reaction at all.

"What about you, huh? How old are you?"

"Thirty-six," he says matter-of-factly with an odd look on his face.

"Wow. You're younger than you look. Those gray hairs were pretty deceiving," I deadpan.

"I do not have gray hairs," he runs his hand over his hair as if checking to see if he can feel said hairs.

"Really, though, when we met I figured you were barely thirty."

"Nope, much, *much* older than that." He speaks quietly, but there's an intensity in his face I can't quite name.

"Thirty-six isn't that old. Besides, age is just a number. My brother is forty and he still makes mud pies in the backyard to throw at me every time he comes over."

He raises a questionable brow, but there's humor in his eyes along with something else that's making my stomach flutter.

"Seriously. I wish I was kidding. I probably still have some in my hair from last night," I chuckle awkwardly, unsure how to respond to the way he's looking at me. Refusing to acknowledge the heat in his gaze or the way his folded arms are making his biceps bulge.

"Anyway, we'll get things resolved quickly, I already put a rush order in for new windows, which we will, of course, pay for. So, no need to worry there."

"I'm not worried in the slightest. I have faith you'll get it all figured out. Thanks for the heads up."

He smiles softly and stuffs his hands in his pockets, perfectly relaxed.

I stand there, at a loss for words. His kindness and generosity in this moment overwhelming. I wasn't kidding when I said people usually yelled at me. I've been cursed at, screamed at and so much more in the past when I had to deliver bad news. It's crazy the way people will talk to you when they see you as nothing but a construction worker or someone on their payroll.

But Wyatt is different.

I adjust my glasses, "Well, I have to get back to work, but I wanted to make sure you were informed. If you have any other questions, let me know. You should get inside, it's cold out here."

"Hear it might even snow tonight."

"Oh, I hope so! I love the snow, but I doubt it. October might be a bit too early."

He shrugs. "You never know. Crazier things have happened."

He looks at me with a glint in his eye and I'm about to ask what kind of crazy things when he asks, "Do you need any help today?"

"You're not busy?"

"I have some time," he shrugs and I swear there's a slight blush on his face.

I can't stop the grin that takes over my face. "Get your gloves, Mr. Reed. We're installing a urinal."

chapter seventeen
wyatt

I don't know what stupid voice in my head convinced me to offer help. The only thing I've ever built in my life is a swing set for Lincoln and Walker had to fix it after the swing fell off. With Lincoln on it. He was fine, it wasn't even two feet off the ground, but proof that I know absolutely nothing about building.

I should've learned my lesson when I offered to help her with the sign a couple weeks ago and I hit her in the stomach with a 2x4. The first time in my whole life I've ever even held a 2x4. She laughed through the pain, which shouldn't even surprise me at this point, and went back to the task at hand.

I don't know how much help I am as we stand in front of a urinal, but I stay nonetheless and watch her work.

"How long have you been doing this?" I ask as I watch her loosen a pipe with a tool I wish I knew the name of.

"Installing urinals?" she grunts slightly with the turn of what I believe to be some kind of wrench, trying to loosen the pipe. "This is only my second time."

"I mean, all of it, you seem to know how to do everything."

"I still have a lot to learn, but I'd like to think I know a little bit about everything."

"How long have you been working for your dad?"

"Officially," she says with even more of a grunt as she pulls the pipe loose, water dripping slightly onto the floor, "since I was sixteen. I started bookkeeping for him. But I've been on construction sites for pretty much as long as I can remember."

"My sister-in-law is the same. She can fix almost anything just from watching her dad growing up."

"Yeah, a lot of it is actually pretty simple once you have a good set of tools and you do it once or twice."

She puts her tool back into her tool belt and stands right in front of the urinal, almost as if she's about to use it. "This is usually where it gets gross."

She shoots me a grin over her shoulder before she squats before the urinal, her face practically in it.

"Yeah, that's disgusting."

She positions herself just right before she lifts it off the wall with graceful ease, and places it on the floor behind her while I stand there watching, unable to do anything.

I've never felt more useless.

"There, not so bad. Now we have to hang that one and then put the pipe back on and voila!" Her arms shoot out and her grin covers her whole face.

"I think you might enjoy this too much."

She giggles. "I like working with my hands."

"Yeah, I can see that," I smile back. "This is just...surprising."

"Why? Cause I'm a woman."

"No," I say defensively. "Women can work in construction."

"I'm glad you agree."

"But have you seen yourself? You're what, ninety-pounds soaking wet and you just lifted a urinal by yourself? You have to see how shocking that is."

"My small stature has definitely gotten in my way before, but I've learned to adapt. Not sure if you noticed, but my boots have lifts in them," she sticks her steel toed boots out for me to see. "The extra height gives me secret advantages."

She stands straighter, hands on her hips, teasing in her gaze.

"You're very strong, Lucy Snow."

It's supposed to be a joke, but something in my tone has her features softening as her smile becomes shy.

"What about you? Mr. Six-Foot-Million. You should be moving urinals."

"Six-four."

"Wow," she mumbles, taking me in from head to toe.

I shoot her a grin and wink. "If you think I'm attractive, you can just say it."

"Does the eyebrow waggle and smirk usually sweep women off their feet?" she says through giggles.

"Yes," I say honestly.

"Well, it's not going to work with this one, Mr. Reed." The formal name stops me in my tracks. Her intentional way of stopping the flirting, but the glint in her eye tells me she doesn't want me to stop.

"I wouldn't expect it too," I cross my arms over my chest. "The professionalism."

"Yes, the professionalism. Now help me put the new urinal in."

"Words I never thought I'd hear. I don't think I'm much help," I chuckle.

"You just have to lift it and hang it on those hooks," she points to two hooks on the wall.

"Remind me why we're switching these out again?" I ask as I stare at the new, shiny urinal at my feet.

"So they all match. We installed a new one in the family bathroom we added up front, but we wanted it all to match. I couldn't find the same exact model, so we just bought new ones in here. We got a deal, so it worked out."

"So I just have to hang it on those hooks?" I motion toward said hooks in the wall and she nods once, trying to hide her grin. She's not succeeding.

"Just laugh already," I say as I bend down to lift the urinal. It's heavier than I anticipated. I'm halfway to the wall wondering how on earth she lifted this by herself.

I make it to the wall, a trip that seemed much shorter when I was empty handed.

"That's it, just line it up," she encourages.

"I can't really see them."

"Here," she says from somewhere beside me and suddenly, I feel her hand on my arm as she guides me toward the hooks. Together we get it lined up and hang it.

"You did it!" she cheers with a clap of her hands.

My arm is still warm from where she wrapped her small fingers around it and I can't believe I'm getting excited over a woman in a men's bathroom while she installs a urinal.

Life sure has its way of surprising you.

"Did you not grow up in a fix-it household?" she asks as she places the pipe back and starts to tighten.

"No really. My mom could be handy with a few things here or there, " I lean one shoulder against the wall as she works, "but we usually hired out."

"Your dad wasn't very handy, then?" she turns back toward me.

I shrug and surprise myself when I say, "I wouldn't know. He left when I was nine."

"Oh," she says quietly, leaning on the wall next to me.

"Sorry. I didn't mean to just...drop that information like that. I don't really talk about it much, but it is what it is."

"Can I ask what happened?"

I take a deep breath and for some unknown reason, I find it easier to say the words than it's ever been before. "He found his secretary more interesting than his family and decided to start a new family with her."

I catch her eye and wait for the pity to show or the 'I'm so sorry' to pour from her mouth, as they always do when people find out the truth. The stories I tell have changed over the years. Various concoctions from he worked overseas so he was never home, to the extreme version where he died in a car accident. I have spun many tales about my life to avoid those sad head tilts and apologies, but she surprises me when she forcefully says, "What a butthead."

Her eyes widen as if she's just as surprised by the words coming out of her mouth. "I'm sorry, that was extremely insensitive, sometimes I don't think before I speak, I should really work on – "

She stops mid-sentence when a laugh bursts from my mouth.

"Please don't apologize, that was probably the best response I've ever gotten from anyone. I hate when people apologize for something they had no hand in or feel sorry for me." I brush her arm with my fingers quickly. "You're right, he is a butthead."

Her smile is tentative, but she doesn't break eye contact. "Do you talk to him at all?"

"No. My brother did for a little bit after he left, but I don't think anyone has heard from him in years."

"But you're close with your mom?"

I nod.

"Is your brother the oldest?"

"No, Winnie is the oldest. Then Walker, then me."

"Winnie, Walker, and Wyatt?" her eyes sparkle and the corner of her mouth lifts.

"Yes, all 'W's. Mom did that on purpose. Thought it was cute."

She giggles, "My mom, too. My siblings and I are all 'L's. Luke, Logan, Landon and Lucy."

"You have three brothers?"

"Yup! Baby of a bunch of boys, though I'd argue they're the bigger babies *most* the time."

We laugh together in the men's bathroom of an empty restaurant. Before I know it, we've fallen into an easy banter, finding comfort in simple conversation. I feel like there isn't a topic we don't cover. We talk about our childhood and how I spent most of my time in football while she spent hours in her backyard building small towns with sticks.

"I was so obsessed with construction as long as I can remember. In the sixth grade, I built an entire city out of recycled bottles for a science fair project that was all about saving the planet. I got second place."

"Who got first."

"Jenny," she rolls her eyes. "Which is totally unfair because she paid a kid in the grade above us to build her a robot."

My eyebrows raise and she just laughs. "It makes sense when you get to know her."

"You guys are close?"

"Oh, yeah, my best friend. We're only a few days apart and we grew up together. More like sisters than cousin's, honestly."

"You're really close with your family," I say, more of a statement than a question.

"Yeah, some could even say too close," she scoffs. "But they're my ride or die. I don't know where or what I would be without them."

"Same," I reply quietly. "I definitely wouldn't be here if it wasn't for Walker. He's been good to me. Too good sometimes."

"What does that mean?"

I run a hand down my face wondering how much I'm willing to share in this echoing bathroom with a girl I just met four weeks ago. A girl who's supposed to be renovating said bathroom and already knows more about my personal life than I've shared with anyone in years.

I turn my head to catch her eyes which I find wide and eager to hear more. Her safety glasses are tossed to the side and I realize it's the first time I've seen her without any glasses on. Her eyes are even bigger than I thought, and somehow brighter in these poor florescent lights. They look almost green, a little turquoise and suddenly the words start coming out with ease.

"I went through a pretty, uh, rough patch in college and most everyone shut me out. My mom wouldn't even let me in the house for a while. I don't blame her, she was alone and scared, I wasn't...in a very good place," I chance a look at her from the corner of my eye and her focus is on me and me alone, listening intently.

"Anyway," I look back at the ground. *"Very* long story short, Walker never gave up on me. Took a bit of time, but we're pretty close now."

She nudges me with her shoulder until I look at her. There's no judgement looking back at me, no pleading for more gory details. She simply says, "Family's important."

"Yeah," I smile. "They are."

Her smile is easy, her features soft. Her eyes have mine in a vice grip. I couldn't look away if I wanted to.

Her gaze shifts down slowly, eyeing my mouth before shooting back up. She looks surprised that she let herself catch a glance, but she doesn't move away. In fact, I feel her lean into me just enough to make her brush my chest every time she takes a breath.

Her lips are just a millimeter away. Her breath is minty fresh as she breathes heavily. Everything in me is telling me to kiss her. To close the space between and take what I've wanted since the first time she opened that blue binder. Heck, since I saw her on the street before I even learned her name.

Forget the restaurant and professionalism and responsibility.

Forget all of it.

Forget anything but her.

I lift my hand to her waist and her small gasp as my fingertips graze her side confirms that there is nowhere else I'd rather be. Nothing else I'd rather be doing.

My lips are just about to meet hers when a sudden cough has us breaking apart.

"Apologies for interrupting," Walker says with a smug smile on his face. "I tried your cell, but you didn't answer, so I figured I'd just stop by."

"No worries," I run my hands on my jeans and I see Lucy shove her glasses back onto her nose. "What's up?"

"Can we talk in the office?" he asks, looking between me and Lucy.

"Oh, uh," I look to Lucy who waves her hand at me.

"I got this. I can do the other one by myself." She sounds calm as can be, but her face is beet red and her eyes a bit too wide.

"You sure?"

She nods. "Yup! I'll grab one of the guys to help if I need anything.

"Alright. I guess, I'll, uh, I'll see you tomorrow?"

"Yes. Tomorrow we paint. Very exciting," she giggles and a smile returns to my face. Something that seems to be happening more and more lately.

"It's good to see you, Lucy," Walker says and she offers him a smile and a "You too," before turning her attention back to the forgotten task.

I follow Walker silently through the dining room and it's not until we step into the office that he turns so quickly on his heel I almost run into him.

"Look, I know what you're going to say – "

"So, you're a plumber now?" he motions to the glasses on my face.

"Okay, not what I thought you were going to say," I remove the glasses from my face. "I was just helping her out. They were short staffed today."

He raises a disbelieving brow. "You were helping? Install toilets?"

"Urinals, and don't sound so surprised."

"Do you even know what a crescent wrench is?"

I roll my eyes. "Did you come here for a reason?"

"Oh right, yeah," he fumbles. "I needed a, um...I wrote up a new job description for the kitchen if you can post it on the website. I want to start interviews sooner rather than later so we're fully staffed by the time we reopen. Also, the shipment I tried to cancel of salmon was not actually cancelled, so we have a hell of a lot of salmon delivering tomorrow."

"You drove all the way over here when I didn't answer the phone to tell me about salmon?" I question.

"Yeah," he replies matter-of-factly.

"I don't buy it."

"What's to buy? We run a business, Wyatt, I'm supposed to keep you informed."

"A text message would've sufficed," I cross my arms over my chest, trying to figure out his motives. "And you know how to post the job listings, so I don't know why you need me to do that."

We stare each other down until he finally runs an exasperated hand down his face. "Fine, Dannie sent me over here because she wanted to know how...things were going."

"What things?"

He gives me a pleading look that says, 'please don't make me admit this.'

Realization suddenly hits. "She sent you to spy on me and Lucy?"

He doesn't respond.

"And you listened to her?"

"You know there isn't any arguing with Dannie," he throws his arms up in exasperation. "Especially pregnant Dannie! At least I didn't sneak any pictures of the two of you like she originally requested."

I quickly shut the office door behind me as his voice rises. "There's nothing going on between me and Lucy."

"That's not what it looked like when I got here."

"I was helping her."

"With your mouth?"

"I didn't do anything."

"You would have done something if I hadn't walked in."

"It's nothing, Walker."

"Look, Wyatt. I'm not one to lecture about dating at work. I mean, I was Dannie's boss for crying out loud. If you really like this girl, it's okay to do something about it. From what I saw, it didn't really look like she was upset about it."

"I was just helping her install – "

"Urinals." He rolls his eyes. "Yeah, I know. You've said that word more in the last two minutes than you've ever said it in your life. Isn't that a bit of a safety concern? The last thing I need is you hurting someone and *I* get sued."

"First of all, Lucy wouldn't sue anyone, she doesn't do business like that and second of all, it's *our* property, I can do whatever I want."

"You sure say her name a lot for someone who isn't interested."

"What does that even mean?"

"It means, you don't know anyone's name, Wyatt. We have employees who have been here for years whose names you don't know. Then comes Lucy and I've heard nothing but her name coming from your mouth. It's not the contractor or the builder or Miss Snow. It's *Lucy.*" He draws out her name dramatically as if mimicking me.

"I sound nothing like that. And you're starting to sound a lot like Ellie," I deflect, but in the back of my mind I know he's right. I know how easily I slip her name into meaningless conversations just for an excuse to say it.

"I know it's none of our business, man, but Dannie has a point," he says, all jokes aside. "I've never seen you look at someone the way you look at her."

"Walker, you guys are reading way too much into things. I barely know this girl. Sure, she's beautiful so maybe there's a little...infatuation there, but it's nothing more. It's just business."

He scoffs. "Yeah, that's what I used to tell myself about Dannie. Infatuated by a beautiful woman, nothing more." He looks me dead in the eye. "It's always more, Wyatt."

"Well, Lucy isn't Ellie."

"No, she's not," is all he says, but I feel a deeper meaning hidden behind those words. Something that tells me that's the whole point.

"How is Ellie?" I change the subject.

He groans. "Oh, you know. Dannie is naturally grumpy, but add back pain, swollen ankles, nausea and no sleep into that. Insufferable is the word you're thinking of. She yelled at me this morning for breathing too loudly while doing the dishes. Pregnant Dannie is a person no one should have to deal with more than once in their life and for some reason I signed up for round two," he chuckles at his joke that should be just that, a joke, but that familiar lump starts to form in my throat and I can feel my face fall.

I don't know anything about pregnant Dannie.

Because I wasn't there.

He registers my silence for what it is and clears his throat awkwardly.

"Anyway, she's just getting a little antsy. I told her I'd pick up some pizza on my way back. I should probably head home before my phone starts ringing off the hook.

I nod, my voice stuck on that lump I can't seem to escape.

"Look, Wyatt, I'm sor – "

"Don't," I stop him. I'm so sick of all the apologies from people who've never done anything wrong. "Please, Walker, just don't."

He looks like he wants to say more on the subject but finally thinks better of it. "Well, feel free to stop by on your way home if you want some pizza. Lincoln would be excited to see you."

He opens the office door, but stops halfway through the doorway to look back at me. "You're not him, Wyatt."

"Who?" I ask.

"The person that you used to be. Start giving yourself some credit. Don't avoid the future because you're scared of repeating the past."

He leaves then, the office door swinging shut behind him.

chapter eighteen
lucy

The tiles make it in an overnight delivery and before we know it the new bathroom is finished.

No more urinal talk for me. How disappointing.

I don't see much of Wyatt in the following week, which has me in my head far too much. We had a great day in the bathroom (words I never thought I'd utter in my life). Really great, actually. Not only was it the easiest conversation of my life, but the feel of his hand grazing my hip and his breath on my face is something I can't forget no matter how hard I try.

Not that I'm trying that hard.

It was extremely unprofessional. I shouldn't have let it get as far as it did, but who could resist Wyatt Reed when he looks at you like that?

He made one of the most stressful days into one of the most relaxing somehow.

Wyatt has a calming presence about him. His voice soothing. He speaks slowly, carefully considering each word before he says it. He listens with intent like he doesn't want to miss a single word.

He's a client, I remind myself. I've lost count of how many times I've repeated those words in my mind.

With the restaurant now remaining closed, we're able to catch up to our schedule by only working a couple days of overtime. By the time the weekend rolls around I'm exhausted and am thankful for a day of no plans and relaxation.

At least, that's what I think until I walk through the door on Friday after work.

"We're going out," Jenny shouts from her room before I've even stepped through the door way.

"But I just got in." I argue.

"We haven't been out in ages and there's a new bar on main that has live music."

"But I don't drink."

"Well, maybe you should start." She tosses a piece of clothing at me from her room. "Wear that."

"Jenny, I don't know. Bars aren't really my scene."

"We're just going for the music. I promise we won't stay long."

"Going at all is staying too long."

"Live a little, Lucy."

She steps out of her room in an extremely short pink skirt and an almost see-through black blouse tucked, the buttons shimmering in the light.

"Who in the world are you trying to impress?"

"No one."

"Liar."

She groans. "Fine, this guy on the dating app is in the band and we've been talking for a while and he asked if I wanted to come see him play. I need a wing woman."

I chuckle. "Well, why didn't you just say so?"

"Because I'm meeting a stranger on the internet at a bar to see his garage band play. I've reached a new level of pathetic."

"Well, then, I'll be pathetic with you."

Her eyes light up. "Really? You'll go?"

"Yes, but only if you let me wear what *I* want to wear."

"Fine, get your pencil skirt and blouse buttoned to your neck and let's go."

wyatt

I've been standing in front of my fridge for about ten minutes, trying to determine what I can make with an old lemon, baking soda and coconut water, when my phone dings.

I grab my phone off the counter and see a notification from an unknown number.

The first thing I see is a photo of a urinal.

Unknown number: Urinals are a beaut.

Unknown number: This is Lucy by the way.

Unknown number: My work phone died so I'm using my personal.

Three dots appear, telling me she's still typing, but I respond before she finishes.

Wyatt: So glad you told me who you were. I wouldn't have any idea who would be texting me bathroom pictures otherwise.

Lucy: It could be a serial killer front, you never know.

Wyatt: Oh yeah, the urinal killer.

Wyatt: But seriously, I'm starting to be concerned by the amount of times I've heard you say that word.

Lucy: Hey, you can never be too cautious of the item-that-shall-not-be-named killer.

I laugh as I drop myself on my bed, the thought of dinner completely forgotten.

Lucy: Anyway, that's not really why I text you. I just got an email that a vendor is running a deal for us on some fabric. The nook bench was finished today so we can order cushions if you want a deal.

Lucy: It's a standard size, so if you want to order them later, no problem. Just wanted you to know I could get them 20% off wholesale. They give us a promo code every year.

She text me on a Friday night at 9pm to tell me about nook cushions? From her personal cell number?

I try not to read too much into this.

I'm unsuccessful.

Wyatt: If you wanted to talk to me, you could just text me. You don't need to come up with a front about cushions Miss Snow.

Lucy: Your flirting energy would be better spent elsewhere, Mr. Reed.

Wyatt: Debatable. It seemed pretty well spent in the bathroom.

I question whether I should send the message. Neither one of us has mentioned the almost kiss and I don't know if that's because she doesn't know what to say or she wants to forget it, but before I can think too hard about it I press send.

Lucy: That wasn't my fault. I was high on item-that-shall-not-be-named work. That really gets me going. You caught me at a really good time.

Lucy: Lucky you.

Wyatt: I must be the luckiest man alive, then.

Lucy: I meant what I said, Wyatt. We need to keep things professional.

Wyatt: Is that why you're texting me about work at 9pm on a Friday night?

Lucy: For your information, I am currently at a bar listening to a local band.

Wyatt: And texting me.

The three dots appear and disappear. Then appear and disappear about five more times before they stop all together.

I can almost see her pushing her glasses up her nose.

Lucy: If you'd like to order cushions with our discount, just let me know. I will send you the link to the website so you can pick a pattern.

Wyatt: You can just pick one. I know nothing about fabrics.

Lucy: Are you sure? I wouldn't want to overstep.

Wyatt: I don't think you can overstep with cushions.

Lucy: Oh you can 100% overstep with cushions. Just ask my Aunt Janice.

Wyatt: I'm afraid to ask.

Lucy: You should be.

Lucy: Anyhoo, just look it over and either I can order it for you or you can just order directly. Whatever you prefer.

Wyatt: I'd prefer you to pick it out and order it.

Lucy: I'll email you the link and you can order it with my promo code.

Lucy: Sent!

Lucy: Goodnight Mr. Reed.

Wyatt: Goodnight Miss Snow.

I drop my phone on my nightstand with a stupid smile on my face.

I don't remember the last time I got excited about texting a girl. There was one a few years ago, but it didn't last long when I wasn't interested in 'casual.'

But even then, nothing has felt like this.

I eat my cold cereal, not even caring that my fridge is practically bare and when I finally slide into bed. I fall asleep without effort and dream of short blondes with sassy attitudes and blue binders.

chapter nineteen
wyatt

It's snowing the first day of November. I think nothing of it as I walk into the office. I grabbed my favorite green sweater from the back of the closet and drove to work like I always do, parking in the spot I always park in. The day was just like any other.

Until she walked in.

There wasn't anything special about the way she was dressed. She had on her work boots and safety glasses, blue binder in hand and work belt sinched. She was wearing blue jeans that had all kinds of dirt and grime on them, but it was the sweatshirt that caught my attention.

It was an NYU sweatshirt. The front had a small NYU written in school colors and the back had a number on it like a football jersey. And not just any number. My number.

Number twenty-three. I chose the letter because W is the twenty-third letter in the alphabet. Everyone on the team called me W and the sweatshirt takes me back in an instant.

It's not like she was wearing *my* jersey. A lot of people have worn that number since I left and even more long before. For all I knew, she didn't even care about the number.

But there was something about it that had me stopping in my tracks and Walker's words repeating in my mind.

Don't avoid the future because you're scared of repeating the past.

I've been avoiding anything and everything as long as I can remember. I'm a master-avoider. I avoided the topic of my dad after he left. I would leave the room anytime his name was mentioned. Even now I hate talking about him.

I would avoid the questions Ellie constantly threw my way about how much I'd had to drink the night before or if I had finished my school assignments.

I avoided Walker's phone calls after he'd lent me money and I couldn't pay him back.

Avoid, avoid, avoid. It's like I didn't know how to do anything else.

But something about that moment – seeing Lucy in my jersey number – made me rethink everything. And the last thing I wanted to do was avoid her.

So I walked up to her.

It wasn't a ground-breaking moment. I think I talked about the weather, I don't really remember. But I remember the feeling of taking the step forward and going after what I wanted with no reservations.

And that's what I've been doing since.

For the last three weeks I've been taking tiny steps forward and refusing to think about what's behind me.

It's been the most exciting time of my life.

I haven't decided if that's pathetic or not. I've moved past hiding in my car from a five-foot blonde, so I like to think I've made progress.

Lucy is calm. A word I don't think she'd use to describe herself and one I think most people wouldn't understand. She speaks loudly when she gets excited, she giggles constantly, sound always emanating in some capacity from her lips. She giggles at herself often and asks herself questions when she thinks no one is around.

Some might find the constant noise irritating, but I find it peaceful. It's so different than the hustle and bustle of the busy restaurant and vastly different from the stark silence of my apartment. It's inviting. It's like simple reminders that she's there if I need someone to talk to.

I've grown too comfortable with it. There's a constant reminder in my brain that this woman is nothing more than a vendor whose paycheck I'll have to sign.

But we all know that's not the truth.

She's much more than that.

And I have no idea what to do about that.

The almost kiss has not been brought up since our text conversation. Not that it was really even brought up then.

She eyed my mouth a little too long when I showed up at the restaurant the next day, but never said a word. I would've brought it up if I knew what to say.

Instead, we moved on like nothing happened, leaving the tension of the kiss sitting pretty between us. Somehow growing thicker with time.

I feel crazy thinking about a girl I hardly know like this. But at the same time, it feels like I've known her forever. I know more about her than I know about anyone.

She never has a shortage of things to say. I don't think she's trying to fill the silence with useless information, she genuinely finds interest in everything and everyone. Constantly curious.

Like a couple days ago when she showed up once again in that NYU sweatshirt and had to ask me about new light fixtures in the family bathroom because what we had in the other was out of stock. Somehow that simple question turned into twenty minutes about our hobbies.

"Running is probably my only hobby," she said, absentmindedly flipping through the lighting catalogue. "Besides sanding of course." She giggled at herself.

It's the most addicting sound. I've found myself asking her dumb questions about what she's doing just so I can hear it.

"I just like being outside and pushing myself, I guess," she continued. "Nothing is better than running just a second faster than I did the day before. It's like kicking my own butt."

I did my best to avoid thinking about her butt as I took the catalogue from her.

"What about you? Any hobbies?"

I shook my head. "Not really. Just hanging with my nephew."

"He's five, right?

"Yeah."

"That's such a fun age. My oldest brother has four kids. The youngest is five and she's just adorable. They say the funniest things and their imagination's always running wild." She pushed her glasses up her nose. I don't even think she does it on purpose. It's almost a reflex. "But is that really a hobby?"

"For me it is."

She looked at me then with a slight tilt in her head, her eyebrows bunched together. "There's nothing you do for fun; just for yourself? Music, sports, anything?"

I don't talk about the past. No one really knows I used to play football except my family. But for some reason it was easy for me to look at her bright eyes and say, "I used to play football. In college."

Her eyebrows went up. "You played college football? That's cool. Where?"

"NYU," I replied pointing at her sweatshirt. "Twenty-three was my jersey number."

"Ha!" she looked down at her sweatshirt. "What a coincidence. What position?"

"Tight end."

"I wish I knew what that meant. I know nothing about sports. I usually did homework when I went to my brother's high school games," she giggled at herself.

Every day since I've learned something new about her. That she hates asparagus and thinks summer is overrated.

"I mean, what adult likes summer? We're not spending our days in swimsuits running around in the water, eating unlimited amounts of popsicles and ice cream sandwiches. We're working in the heat and sweating uncontrollably, while simultaneously trying to fit into our bathing suits and prohibiting any sugar loaded treat. It's horrible. Winter is my favorite. Especially the snow," she giggles for the millionth time and you think I'd be sick of it, but I'm not.

I learned on a Friday afternoon that she watches *I Love Lucy* reruns on repeat. "I mean, it's a bit cliché with my name being Lucy and all, but it never gets old. Have you seen it? It's so good!"

On a Monday morning I discovered she hates breakfast food. "Pancakes are nothing but flour and sugar, which you then cover in sugary syrup. Talk about a clogged artery waiting to happen. That's not to say I don't love sweet things. I can throw back a king size candy bar like you wouldn't believe. Just not for breakfast. Which is essentially what you're doing when you eat a stack of pancakes."

The Friday after Thanksgiving she came in to paint the nook bench and I learned she hates Turkey. "I know I sound like a little negative nelly, but I will never understand what's so great about Thanksgiving food. We pick the driest meat on planet earth, combined with even dryer stuffing. The rolls are pretty great, but after about three you feel so puffy you can't eat anything else. Though, I will say, my mom makes the best pumpkin pie ever!"

Every day, no matter how hard I try, my feet move of their own accord to wherever she is, just to hear what she has to say. I've never been one to shy away from speaking, but with her I don't care to say anything. There's peace to be found in simply listening, not feeling any pressure to carry a conversation. Not feeling the need to offer a silly anecdote or some philosophical idea about a topic you don't actually know anything about.

Before I left yesterday, I caught her just outside my office, doing inventory on new parts.

"Any fun plans for the weekend?" I asked.

"Just the usual," she said with a checkmark in her notebook. "*I Love Lucy* and bed by nine."

"It's a Friday night, you're not going to another bar?"

She looked at me then. "That was a one-time thing. I like my apartment, I like my shows and I *really* like my pajamas. That is the perfect Friday night for me. What about you? You going to any ragers this weekend?"

I chuckle at her choice of words. "Ragers is a bit extreme. I'll probably go to Walker's house and play *Candyland* for the millionth time with Lincoln. I still can't figure out how to win at that game."

She smiles. "There's no figuring it out, it's all luck."

"Yeah, I have none of that."

"So not a party person?"

I shake my head. "Not at all."

She stares at me with pinched brows.

"Is that bad?"

"No," she shakes her head. "Just surprising."

"Why is that so surprising?"

She shrugged. "College football player, thirty-five-year-old single man living alone just a half hour from New York City. I don't know, I just figured you went out a lot."

"I used to, but that didn't usually turn out too good."

"Oh, right," she nodded once. "The 'rough patch'."

"Yeah, the rough patch."

"You know, I think it's really cool that you got your life together. I know a lot of people who sit around doing the same thing over and over again. It takes a lot of humility to do what you did."

I scoffed slightly. "I wouldn't say things like that unless you know the whole story."

"I don't need to know the whole story. I know who you became at the end of the story. Who you are now. That's the only part of the story I care about."

The words fell from her lips with a heavy intensity and she let them sit in the air for a beat before she turned and left me alone.

It was those words she left me with that played on repeat last night, making me never want to wake up.

By the last Saturday in November, only one week before renovations end, I get a text from Ellie at five in the morning asking if I'd be willing to keep Lincoln overnight for them to go on a last-minute babymoon. Whatever that means. Before I even got a chance to respond, my doorbell wrang where I found Lincoln on my doorstep with a backpack and Walker halfway down the stairs calling, "Thanks again!" over his shoulder.

I barely got the kid through the door before he asked for ice cream. It was only six in the morning. I managed to divert the ice cream talk with a promise that after the park and breakfast, we could potentially stop at the drug store and pick up a pint for us to eat after dinner. And by potentially, he knows I mean that's absolutely what we're doing.

We've been at the park for over two hours now and he hasn't stopped moving. Running, running, running, 24/7 and never tiring.

"Lincoln, that's too far," I call for the tenth time. He'd run away and never come back if I'd let him. I swear he's going to be a track star when he's older. He just never stops.

He turns around and runs back to me, his breathing extremely uneven when he asks, "Did you see how fast I was?"

"Yeah, crazy fast. But you can't go that far."

He nods quickly before running again.

We spent the first half of our time at the park playing tag, his favorite game. Then we kicked a soccer ball around for a little bit before he wanted to race to the parking lot and back. We've been running for an hour and a half. I'm so worn out I had to convince him to let me take a break. I found a park bench to drop myself onto as he continued to run.

He run's back and forth in circles chasing pigeons and pretending to fly like a bird. "Look, Wyatt, I can fly!" he yells, flapping his arms, running as fast as he can.

It's exactly how I was when I was little.

Mom says she never could keep me still. It's part of the reason she put me in football so young. Just something for me to do that allowed me to get the jitters out as she called them. I'd play football for hours and then go home and run around the backyard. I ran around the house so much, she claims I wore out paths in the carpet. I haven't seen said paths, but I remember getting yelled at a lot for running in the house.

It's hard to see how much he resembles me.

I feel the all too familiar ache in my chest forming when I suddenly hear, "I told him I had to think about it."

I'd recognize that voice anywhere. Somehow in the short amount of time we've spent together, I've memorized every cadence of every word. Her voice is so soft, but also firm without being loud or abrasive.

I turn instantly toward the sound and can almost see Walker's smug grin in my head that I noticed her so quickly.

She's standing behind me, talking on the phone. She's facing me, but looking at the ground, pinching the bridge of her nose.

"Mom, I didn't say no. I said I had to think about it."

Her hand drops to her side and her eyes closed in frustration. She looks like she's at the end of her patience, but her voice is as soft as ever. Never rising, never frustrated. Always gentle.

She nods a couple times, biting her bottom lip, as she listens. "Mom, I'm at the park, okay, I have to go."

She offers a few "yeah," and "sure thing, Mom," before finally hanging up the phone.

She doesn't see me staring, her eyes are closed and she's taking deep breaths. I take the time to admire the bright blue leggings she chose along with a long sleeve, tight black shirt.

I could say I agreed to bring Lincoln to the park without a single thought that Lucy might be here for her Saturday run, but I'm not a liar.

"You should take a picture, it lasts longer."

My eyes immediately shoot to hers. Her hands are on her hips and a single eyebrow raised, but the smile she's trying to fight is all I notice.

I grin. "You got a camera?"

She laughs once. "You're such a flirt."

"Only with you."

She blushes bright red, pressing her finger to her glasses, pushing them up her nose.

I take a glance at Lincoln who's still running in circles before I stand and move next to her.

"Are you okay?" I ask, shoving my hands in my pockets.

"Yeah, why wouldn't I be?" she brushes a wayward strand from her face.

"I overheard your conversation."

She sighs. "It's just my mother."

"It sounded kind of intense."

"It's nothing, really."

"It didn't sound like nothing."

She looks at me for a moment, contemplating before sighing in defeat. "She's upset because she wants me to go out with this doctor guy and I don't want to. I mean, I've seen the guy pee on a tree for crying out loud. I don't really want to date him."

"When in the world did he pee on a tree?"

She laughs a bright, solid, genuine laugh and I don't think there's anything I wouldn't do, wouldn't say, to hear it again. "We were seven."

"Oh, I guess that's better. So, you've known him for a long time?"

"Yeah, forever. We grew up next door to each other."

"You don't like him?"

She shrugs one shoulder. "Our families are close. He's a really great guy, super nice. I'm just not interested in him like that.

"Nice?" I raise an eyebrow. "So, he's ugly?"

Her mouth pops open in surprise, her blue eyes wide. "He is not ugly. He's really nice. He's just not my type."

"No man wants to be called nice. It's like a slap in the face."

"Why? He's a nice guy."

"Yeah, so was Isaac Newton and he died a virgin."

"That hasn't been confirmed." She looks up through her eyelashes with enough attitude to put an army general to shame.

I take a step closer. "So, just say it; he's ugly."

"No one is ugly, Wyatt."

I scoff avoiding the feeling in my chest when she says my name that way. "Oh, some people are definitely ugly."

"That's not how it works," she argues, crossing her arms.

"How does it work then, Miss Snow?"

She raises an eyebrow at the formal name but continues. "Do you like pickles?"

I frown in confusion. Where is she going with this? "Yes."

"Well, I don't. Does that mean pickles are disgusting?"

"No, pickles are delicious."

"Exactly."

"You've lost me."

"Just because you don't see the value in something doesn't mean it isn't there." She drops her arms to her sides and looks up at me. "Beauty is subjective. For example, other people might find you completely repulsive."

"Other people? " I ask, leaning a little closer. "So, you don't find me repulsive, then?"

Her eyes widen farther than I've ever seen and her mouth opens slightly. She's stunned, unsure where to go from here, but I have to hand it to her because she recovers quickly.

"You're not the worst thing I've ever seen."

I laugh once and her lips twitch like she's trying not to smile. "You're really feisty."

"Only with you," she throws my words back at me with serious attitude.

We've shifted closer. I can see the beads of sweat on her forehead and feel her breath hitting my chin as she looks up at me. I squeeze my hands tightly, doing everything I can not to wrap them around her waist and pull her to me.

She looks up at me over the top of her glasses with the same wide-eyed intensity she gave me in the bathroom when we almost kissed.

My eyes drop to her mouth and I don't even care that we're in the middle of a public park when I hear her intake of breath and her hand reaches out and grabs my bicep.

And then Lincoln scream.

I don't think I just move. I bolt in his direction, as fast as I can, my heart already beating a million miles a minute, terrified of what I'll find. The sound like a knife to my heart, nothing but sheer pain. I find him crumbled in the grass, holding his arm and crying.

"Lincoln, what happened?" I ask as I lower to my knees and pull him into my arms.

"I tripped on the rock...and...I..." His sobs are so rough he can't hardly get the words out. "I...hurt...my...arm."

"It looks like his arm popped out of the socket."

I didn't even realize Lucy had followed until I hear her beside me. I shift him in my lap and check his left arm and he immediately starts crying harder when I try to lift it.

"What do I do?" I ask her.

"You need to take him urgent care. They'll pop it back in." She rubs my arm in reassurance. "It's not a big deal. I've done it a couple times. Hurts terribly, though."

"Right." I lift him with me as I stand and carefully switch him to one arm while I try to pull my phone out of my pocket, but trying to hold him with one arm is difficult when it seems like no matter what I do, it hurts his arm even more and his cries just get louder.

"What do you need?" Lucy asks.

I cradle him back in my arms and hold as tightly as I can. "My phone, it's in my left pocket."

There's a soft blush on her cheeks when she sticks her hand in my pocket and if I didn't have a screaming Lincoln in my ear, I would revel in the way her hand brushes my thigh as she grabs my phone and pulls it out.

"Can you call my brother? The password is zero-seven-zero-four."

She types in my passcode. "Walker, right?" she asks as she scrolls through my contacts.

"Yeah he's on my favorites list."

She finds his name and calls the number as we walk as fast as we can to my car without running or hurting Lincoln more.

"It hurts, Uncle Wyatt," Lincoln whines as I slip him into his car seat.

"I know buddy, I'm sorry. We're going to go to the doctor and they're going to fix it. I promise."

chapter twenty
lucy

Urgent Care is packed.

Poor little Lincoln has been such a trooper, sitting on Wyatt's lap watching videos on his phone eating anything and everything Wyatt could've possibly found in the vending machine. I'm sure it's empty now.

We're in the waiting room for almost an hour when two people hurry through the door and straight to the small boy in Wyatt's arms. I recognize Walker and I assume the tall redhead must be his wife that answered the phone when I called.

"Baby, are you okay?" the woman asks, rubbing his head.

"Uncle Wyatt bought me snacks," he says with a mouthful of cheese crackers.

She chuckles softly. "I see that. How is your arm?"

"It's really bad, Mommy, but I only cried a little bit. Wyatt said I was so brave," his gaze moves to Wyatt. "Right?"

Wyatt nods once, his voice somber. "You were really brave, buddy."

"Wyatt is holding it so I don't move it by accident cause it still hurts. But I'm not crying anymore."

"You're the bravest, sweetie," she kisses the top of his head.

"Any idea how long the wait is?" Walker asks.

Wyatt shakes his head.

His voice is quiet and he hasn't looked at either of the parents since they walked in. He hasn't looked at anything since we sat down. His eyes haven't strayed from Lincoln once.

"I have to pee, Daddy," Lincoln yells loud enough for half the waiting room to hear.

His dad chuckles and carefully takes him from Wyatt's arms.

"Let's find a bathroom, then," he says, carrying him off.

The redhead turns to me once they're out of sight. "I'm Dannie, Lincoln's mom. Thanks for the phone call."

"Oh, of course. Sorry it was a stranger," I chuckle awkwardly. "I'm Lucy."

"Oh," her eyes spark with recognition. "You're the contractor?"

"Yeah, that's me."

"I'm the one that recommended you guys. I'm Abe Brookes' daughter."

"Oh, right. Nice to meet you."

"I remember your dad a little," she smiles. "I was on the job a lot when I was a kid."

"My dad has talked about you. Says he taught you how to throw your first punch."

"That he did," she laughs. "He was a very good teacher."

She turns toward Wyatt and lightly kicks his foot. "Wasn't he? I can throw a pretty mean right hook."

"Yeah," he mumble, barely audible, his eyes still on the ground.

"Wyatt," she kicks his foot again.

He looks up at her, but just barely and mutters the words, "Sorry I ruined your weekend."

"Wyatt," she starts, but he ignores her. She grabs his arm and pulls him up to stand in front of her, Lincoln's half eaten snacks falling to the floor. She's so tall she almost reaches his height. "Everything is fine, Wyatt. Things like this happen."

He pulls her into a hug and kisses the top of her head. "I'm so sorry," he mumbles in a voice that sounds like he might cry.

It suddenly feels too personal for me to be watching and I awkwardly turn around until I'm facing the other direction, watching the old man in the corner argue with his wife about his dentures.

"Wyatt, stuff like this happens," I hear behind me. "He's five. He's bound to break a few bones. And this isn't even a break."

"It wouldn't have happened if he was with Walker."

"Hey," I can hear her slap his arm. "Don't do that. It could have just as easily happened under Walker's watch. Or mine or your moms. This is *not* your fault."

He responds so quietly. "Everything's my fault, Ellie."

I question the nickname for a beat, and the cadence in his voice when he says it.

"Lincoln Reed," a nurse calls out just as Lincoln and his dad come back from the restroom.

I turn just in time to see Dannie squeeze Wyatt's arm once before rushing to Lincoln's side.

"We'll be here," Wyatt says as they follow the nurse through the two-way doors.

He slumps back down in the chair as the door closes behind them.

"Are you gonna wait for them?" I ask, taking a seat next to him.

He doesn't look at me, just nods. "Thanks for your help."

"Of course."

He stares at the door where Lincoln and his parents disappeared through.

"Are you okay?" I ask which sounds incredibly stupid the second it comes out of my mouth. He's clearly not okay, the way his head is drooping down and his shoulders slumped. We're in an urgent care for crying out loud.

"Yeah, you don't have to stay."

I lean back and get as comfortable as I can in the hard hospital chairs. "It's fine. I can keep you company. It could be a while. When I pulled my arm from the socket when I was a kid they did an x-ray and everything. I had to wait a while."

He looks up at me then. "How old were you?"

"Seven or eight. I was playing football in the backyard with my brothers and things got a little out of hand. My oldest brother, Luke, pulled my arm right out of the socket. He still feels guilty about that. Guilt I may or may not use every now and then when necessary," I chuckle and am relieved when he offers a small smile in return.

His eyes catch mine and he murmurs, "You're not what I expected."

There's a weight in his words that I feel in every part of my body.

"What do you mean?" I whisper.

He shrugs. "You're just...bigger than you look?"

That makes me laugh. "Don't know how I feel about the word 'big', but I think I know what you mean."

"I think maybe powerful would be a better word."

I scoff at that one. "Ah, funny."

"I'm serious. You're a force, Lucy Snow."

His eyes lock with mine and there's not a trace of humor in them. It's the levity in his gaze that gives me the courage to ask, "Can I ask you something?"

"Sure."

"The redhead; Dannie was it?"

He nods.

"Is there..." I stumble over the words, not sure how to ask the question that shouldn't be eating at me. "A history there?"

His eyes widen just a bit. "Why do you ask?"

I shrug. "Just seemed kind of...intense. You looked a little sad I guess. I don't know. Sorry if I'm stepping on toes here, I get I'm just the contractor. I'm a nobody," I laugh breathlessly. "I'm just surprisingly good at reading people. My mom says it's a gift." I realize I'm word vomiting on him right now and I close my mouth tightly.

"Well, your mother is right. You are good. And you're not a nobody." He shifts in his seat. "But there's a little bit of a history, yes."

I don't respond, giving him the opportunity to continue or change the subject. Whatever he's more comfortable with.

I take in a breath when he continues.

"We dated in college."

Pretty sure my eyes are wide as saucers. I'm good at a lot of things but hiding my emotions is not one of them. My face says it all. "But she's married to your brother?"

He nods.

"That must make some awkward holiday dinners," I chuckle and am glad when he does too.

He looks down at his hands. "It did for a little bit, but it's good now."

My leg bounces as I think of a million things I want to know, but I know it would be inappropriate to ask. Still, I question, "Do you...still have feelings for her?"

I don't know why the question is so hard to ask. He's a client. It doesn't matter. We shouldn't even be having this conversation. But I find myself holding my breath waiting for his answer.

"Not like that," he shakes his head. "I mean, there was definitely a time when I was working through some...feelings." He shifts uncomfortably, running a hand down his face. "But no. Any feelings I had for Ellie are long gone."

"Then what's the look for?"

"What look?"

"You look at her with this like...longing. Like you're sad almost."

He glances at me out of the corner of his eyes. "Am I that transparent?"

I shrug. "To me you are."

A strange look crosses his face. His eyebrows bunch a little and his mouth sits open like he wants to say something.

"I'm sorry if this is too personal. You don't have to share anything with me." An uncomfortable laugh escapes and I move to stand, but his hand wraps around my forearm gently.

"Don't go," he pleads so quietly I barely hear it.

I look down at his hand on my arm, his thumb rubbing just enough to notice. I sit back in my seat carefully as he squeezes my arm once before letting go and I hate how cold it suddenly feels.

"You're easy to talk to."

I laugh breathlessly. "It's my nosiness. I ask a lot of invasive questions."

He offers me a small half smile and goes on. "I do miss her. But not like you're thinking. I miss things that could've been. I look at her and Walker and Lincoln and I guess I just feel..."

"Jealous?" I offer.

He nods once, eyes on mine again. "I've never told anyone that before. Never really said it out loud."

I place my hand on his hand that's resting on the armrest between us. "It's a fair feeling. Especially with your history with her."

His eyes drop to my hand on his and he mumbles, "You have no idea."

"I get that feeling too sometimes," I say, letting go of his arm. There's a look of disappointment that crosses his face when my hand drops to my lap, but it disappears so quickly I think I imagined it. "I got my undergrad in Construction Management and Architecture and figured I'd take over the family business one day, but things just haven't really gone the way I thought. I worked my butt off working double in college to get all my experience hours with one of the best architects in the city. I took the state test like a week after I graduated college, which is almost unheard of. I did it all perfectly, but..." I look down at my lap and pick lint off my blue leggings. "I haven't done anything with it since. I haven't offered my services, haven't looked at any openings for architects. I don't know, I guess I look at my brothers and all their accomplishments and I feel jealous sometimes."

"Why?"

"Because it seems so easy for them. They went to school, got great jobs, they just did exactly what they wanted, no fear. I wish I could be that brave."

"Lucy, you're the – " he starts, but the words I so desperately want to hear fade away as Walker comes through the double doors interrupting. Wyatt bolts to his feet.

"Is he okay?"

"He's fine. Just popped it out of the socket. He's good now. Handled it like a champ. They told him to wear a sling for a couple days to be safe, but he'll be perfectly fine." He turns to me and smiles. "Thank you for calling and waiting."

"Of course. If you guys need anything, let me know."

"We will, thank you again." He looks back at Wyatt. "He's fine, man. It could've happened under anyone's watch. Don't beat yourself up. He wants to see you. I told him you were still here." He pats him on the shoulder. "Dannie's just signing the paperwork to release him. Do you want to go get ice cream with us?"

Wyatt nods.

"Great. Just wait here, we'll be back."

He's barely down the hall when Wyatt asks, "Do you want to come?"

"Come where?"

"Ice cream."

"Oh," I say like an idiot. He's inviting me to get ice cream with his family? "I don't want to impose."

"You're not imposing."

"Uh, I..." I'm not sure what to say or how to handle this. He's my client. How many times do I have to remind myself of that? I'm going to do something stupid if I'm not more careful. The almost kisses are further than it ever should have gotten.

"I'm sorry. This is unprofessional. You're right. I guess I just..." he trails off again, leaving everything I want to hear unspoken.

"It's okay. I should go, though. Let me know how he is."

"I will."

"Bye, Wyatt."

"Bye, Lucy."

chapter twenty-one
wyatt

"Where's my baby?"

"Here I am," I stand from the couch, arms wide.

My mother pushes past me without even a glance saying, "You're the biggest baby I've ever seen."

I drop my hands on my hips. "I'm not sure how to take that."

"Grandma!" Lincoln yells as he rushes into her arms.

"How is that arm of yours?" she asks and he rushes into a story about his "battle wound" as Walker's been calling it for the last week.

Walker and Ellie ended up taking their trip two days late and I kept Lincoln with me, which kept me too occupied to get to the restaurant. It's been four days since I've seen Lucy and I'm doing my best not to think about how hard that's been. Construction should be done next week and then we'll probably never see each other again.

I shouldn't let myself get attached to someone like this.

I throw my arm around Winnie's shoulders as she comes in, two screaming kids behind her. "I used to be the baby she would rush to see."

"Oh, you're still a baby," she says. "Just in a different way."

"I'm going to choose to not be offended by that remark."

"Oh, no need. Offense was intended," she smiles slyly.

I chuckle as I wrap my other arm around her in a hug. "Where's Brian?"

"Working," she rolls her eyes. "He's always working these days. But the promotion will be worth it. At least, it better be."

"Uncle Wyatt, guess what?" her youngest, Brookelyn, says.

I pretend to think about it for a minute before I respond. This is a game we play every time she sees me these days. "Chicken butt."

She giggles like she always does when I answer her 'guess what' with the timeless classic. Winnie doesn't though. I get a swat on the arm. "I just got her to stop calling the kids at school chicken butts. She got sent to the office three times in one week!"

I laugh, sticking my hands up in defense. "Not my fault. I learned it from Walker."

Brookelyn giggles again and rushes out the door with her brother, Camden. She rarely has anything for me to actually guess. She just thinks chicken butts are hilarious and I'm willing to facilitate her joy.

"I learned it from Winnie," Walker says.

"Interesting," I turn back to Winnie.

"Pretty sure that's a lie, but I'll concede."

Walker gives Winnie a hug, followed by Ellie.

"Thanks for coming," Ellie says. "Lincoln is so excited for everyone to see him play."

"The videos you sent were just amazing," my mom praises as we make our way to the backyard.

"He's getting so good," I agree, wrapping my arm around her. "He's so fast and he has a lot of control. A lot of the kids struggle to continuously kick the ball while running, but he can do it all so well."

"You must be very proud of him," my mom pats my chest with a smile.

"Yeah, I am."

"How's the restaurant?" she says.

"Good. Everything's almost back together, it's looking really good."

"I heard the contractor's pretty great," Winnie chimes in with a smirk.

I shoot a glare at Walker. "Yeah, *Snow Better Builders* is doing a great job."

"Oh, I want to hear, but I need to get the cupcakes in the fridge," my mom says before turning back into the house.

"Really?" I ask Walker in a whisper so my mom doesn't hear from the kitchen. "Are you telling everyone?"

"That you have a crush?" he asks. "Yes."

I roll my eyes. "I do not have a crush."

"You can't take your eyes off her."

"You asked me to oversee the renovation."

"Yeah, the renovation. Not the contractor."

I open my mouth to retort, but my mother comes back and the last thing I need is her meddling in my love life. Not that this is in any way my love life. This is work.

It's just work.

The kids enjoy the snow and Walker braves the cold weather to barbecue hamburgers outside. The kids run, scream, and jump all over the backyard. They don't get to see each other enough. Winnie and Brian moved to Chicago a couple years back and it's been hard to get everyone together since.

Ellie is just passing out Walker's famous strawberry cupcakes that have become a family staple when my phone rings.

"No phones at the dessert table," Ellie chastises.

I check the number and hold my phone for her to see. "It's Lucy."

Her face immediately changes. "Oh, well, that's different."

"Yes, it is," I say from the sliding glass doorway. "Because she's the contractor and she might have a *business* question."

"Yes, of course." She makes air quotes as she says, "Business."

I just roll my eyes and close the door behind me as I step inside the house.

"Hello?"

"Wyatt?"

"Lucy, what's up?"

"Well, there's a, uh..." she trails off, her voice slightly shaky. "There's not a problem, per se," she continues, and I can hear a pen tapping her teeth. "Just a little-teeny-tiny-itty-bitty-baby-hiccup."

I laugh at her words and grab my keys. "I'll be there in ten."

lucy

I've never been more humiliated.

And that's saying something. I'm not the clumsiest person, but I've had my moments. I was voted most likely to break a bone my freshman year of high school because I took one volleyball to the head in P.E. In my defense, the volleyball team was aggressive when we were in open gym and those balls were bigger than my head.

Then there was the debacle at my college graduation party where I accidentally pantsed myself in front of all the guests during Luke's speech about how impressive and professional I was.

So there's been a few embarrassing moments in my time, but nothing beats the look on Wyatt's face when he steps up to the restaurants back door and is immediately faced with the most humiliating moment of my entire existence.

He looks at the mess on the office floor then up to me, gesturing toward said mess. Though, that's probably not a big enough word to describe it. It's much more than a mess.

"Is this the little-teeny-tiny-itty-bitty-baby-hiccup?" he asks.

I nod.

His nose scrunches at the mess. "Is that what I think it is?"

I nod again.

He covers his mouth with a fist as he clears his throat and I realize he's trying to hide his smile. "May I ask how this happened?"

"Those things are not as sturdy as they look!" I point to the toppled over blue enclosure of doom as I will be calling it from this point forward. "We had one come in for the workers because I wanted to leave the nice, expensive, fancy ones for the customers because you guys were originally going to open during the last of the renovations. The crew can easily make a mess and I didn't want them in the same place as the customers."

He chuckles, but quickly covers it with a cough.

"I recognize the irony of that statement considering this is a huge mess." I tuck my hair tighter behind my ears for something to do with my hands. "It's not entirely my fault though. It was in the way on the other side of the building while we were trying to bring in some of the tables and so I had them move it last week when they came to empty it. I figured the dumpster already smells, why not put this by it, you know? But they put it halfway on the curb without realizing it, so it was already off kilter and unstable! I was in a bit of a rush because the painters were here and we're running behind schedule because two guys called in sick the last three days and I wanted to get the painters started because they should've started two days ago," I realize I'm rambling on and talking so fast, I'm not sure if he's following, but I don't think I can stop at this point. "Anyway, I tried to scurry out of there a bit too quickly, but when I went to shut the door, I tripped on the curb and used the open door to catch my fall and well..."

I trail off and look down at the horrible mess in the doorway. Only in my worst nightmares would I knock over a full porta potty into a client's office.

If only I could go back to my pants falling off in the middle of my graduation speech. That was much less humiliating.

"I told them it was too close to the door, but they wouldn't listen!" I drop my hands at my sides so rough, they make a slapping sound on my legs. I'm lucky none of it landed on me.

"You knocked over a porta potty. Into my office." It's not a question, just a statement of fact. I can hear the taunting humor in his tone.

"Yes, and I will get it resolved a-sap! It's just..." I tuck my hair so tight behind my ears I probably look bald. "I'm gonna be honest, this isn't exactly my area of expertise. I've never had to clean up...excrement off the floor."

I immediately face palm not even able to believe the reality of the situation. Or the fact that I just used the word excrement in everyday conversation. Though, I'm not sure tipped over porta potties is an everyday conversation.

Also, I'm going to need to find something to cover my nose because the smell is getting unbearable.

"It's not that bad. It's only part of the floor," he points out. It didn't touch the rug, so that's good. Most of it's outside. At least it didn't get on you." He winks at me and I want to shrivel up and die. "We have a cleaning service that comes in weekly to deep clean the bathrooms. I have an emergency number, I'll call them. Though I would say this is probably a biohazard so we might need to stop construction and close shop until they tell me what we need to do." he says looking around the floor in front of him, checking his pant pockets. "Is the front door open? I don't have my key."

"Oh, yes, you can come around front, I'll unlock it." I shuffle into the dining room and meet him at the front door. He steps through and his hand immediately finds my arm, rubbing soothingly.

"Don't worry about it, Lucy. I'm sure it could, uh...it could happen to anyone."

He's still trying not to laugh and my cheeks are so red I can feel them burning.

"Just laugh already, it's fine."

He chuckles lightly but continues rubbing my arms. "You could laugh, too, you know. It is pretty funny."

I look up at him and his dark eyes are bright and full of humor and a small laugh bubbles out of me. Half humor, half embarrassed.

I groan and drop my face onto his chest in humiliation. So humiliated I can't even enjoy the fact that my face is pressed against his pecks and how firm they are. Or realize how unprofessional this is. "This is the worst moment of my entire life."

"The cleaning crew is going to come and everything will be fine," he rubs my arms, soothingly. "We might need to open the window though, cause the smell is pretty bad."

I groan loud and long. "I need a time machine to turn back time where I don't tip over a stupid porta potty."

"Nah," he shakes his head. "If you hadn't knocked it over, you wouldn't have called me."

I look up at him, his fingers tighten around my arm lightly. "So?"

"So," he says simply. "I wanted to see you today."

chapter twenty-two
wyatt

We had to push the reopen a week.

Something I didn't complain about.

The excrement debacle, as Lucy has been calling it, created a biohazard that we had to call public health officials out for and file a report. She apologized a million times over.

Honestly, it wasn't even that bad. It barely spilled into the office. 90% of it was outside, but any percentage required a report, considering the office is so close to the kitchen. We only had to shut down for three days while it was disinfected and reinspected.

"We are paying for this one," Lucy chastises me over the phone. "This was my fault, we will take full responsibility."

It was late on a Friday night, but I got the bill when I got home and I wanted to let her know everything was settled. I debated calling so late, but the unexplainable need to hear her voice won out and I dialed her number.

She immediately yelled at me once I told her I was paying it.

"Lucy, really, it's totally fine. We can pay for it."

"Nope. Not how it works, so stop arguing with me."

"See?" I smile. "A force."

I can hear a smile in her voice when she says, "Sorry, it pushed us out a week, but we finished everything today. I was actually going to call you. When do you want to get the key?"

"I, uh, I'm free right now?"

"Oh, that actually kind of works. I'm still here."

"Lucy, it's nine o'clock, why are you still there?"

"There were some things I wanted to finish up before I called you."

"Is everyone still there?"

"No, I sent the crew home at six."

"Lucy –"

"Wyatt, just get over here already and let me do my job the way I want to do my job."

"Yes ma'am."

She's standing in front of the door much like the first time I met her. Blue binder in hand. I'm telling you, she sleeps with it.

"You must be the contractor?" I smile as I step out of the car and onto the curb.

She giggles as she closes the distance between us and extends her hand.

I wrap my hand around hers. "I'm Wyatt. You are?"

"Miss Snow," she giggles again.

"So we're back to that, huh?" I squeeze her hand once before releasing it.

"Yes, but if you butter me up enough, I just might let you call my Lucy *and* install some urinals."

"What a dream."

"Well, I guess we should just cut to the chase," she hands me the spare key. "Here's the key. Everything is spotless. Swept and mopped the floors myself and put all the tables back onto the dining room floor. Spick and span."

"Please tell me you didn't put out twenty-five tables and chairs by yourself?"

"Fine," she says turning to open the door. "I won't tell you."

I follow behind her into the dining to find it exactly as she said: spick and span.

"Lucy, this is incredible."

"Isn't it?" She smiles as she moves through the tables toward the expansion. "The private room turned out great."

She opens the door in the far-right corner to a nice rectangular room with a single long table set up down the middle.

"This is amazing. We always just had this awkward corner we didn't know what to do with. Closing it up for a room was a really good idea."

"Thank you," she pushes her glasses up her nose. "But wait until you see the nook bench. I think it's my favorite part."

I turn my attention to the newly added rounded window complete with the bench and a round table in front of it. "This will be really nice for special dinners like anniversaries or birthdays," she says. "I'd say you can fit about eight people around the table. It's kind of hidden a little in the corner, but still part of the dining room."

I nudge her shoulder with mine. "You're just full of good ideas, aren't you?"

"What can I say, I'm brilliant. Now, we just have to get the cushions in."

I take one more look around the room, taking in the space that's almost doubled in size. The tables set up perfectly, with just enough space between each one and the lights strung on the ceiling.

"This is incredible, Lucy," I say when I turn back to her. She's standing close, her hands clasped in front of her. "Congratulations."

"For what?"

"For all of this," I gestured around me. "This is all your doing. Your design, your crew, your everything. It's amazing."

I inch closer slowly, afraid I'll startle her if I move as quickly as I want to.

Her smile softens, getting slightly embarrassed as it always does whenever I compliment her.

"Thank you for picking it," she whispers and before I can think better of it, my hand reaches up and tucks her stray hair behind her ear. Her small intake of breath has me wanting to move her hair back in her face just so I can do it again.

It's that faint gasp and wide eyes that have me placing my hand on her neck and pulling her closer to me. Her hand reaches up and wraps around my wrist and for a beat I think she might push my away, but she tightens her grip on my arm and leans forward.

"Uncle Wyatt!"

I hear Lincoln just before I feel him run into my leg. I bend down to pick him up and look up to find Walker and Ellie standing by the front door.

"What are you doing here?" I ask as they look between Lucy and me. Walker looks like he would rather be anywhere else and Ellie is practically glowing.

"We, uh, thought we'd stop by and check it out on our way to dinner," Walker replies. "I figured the crew and everyone would be gone by now."

"Isn't it past your bedtime?" I tickle Lincoln's stomach.

"I'm not sleepy, though."

"I told him he could go out with us just this once." Ellie says, still smiling.

"Well, I'll probably just head out. I have a couple things I need to load in the truck and then I'll be out of your way," Lucy says.

Before I can even try to stop her she scurries through the dining room and out the front door.

"Are you crazy?" Ellie practically yells when the front door closes behind Lucy.

I put Lincoln back on the floor. "I'm sorry, what did I do?"

"You're just letting her leave like that?"

"What would you like me to do?"

"Go get her for crying out loud!"

"Ellie, please, there's nothing – "

"Don't you dare say there's nothing going on, Wyatt. If we hadn't walked in you two would very much have something going on right now."

I turn to Walker for help. "What about not mixing business with pleasure?"

"Don't look at me. I married my employee."

I roll my eyes. "Weren't you the one that said you were impressed with my desire to remain professional and not cross any lines?"

"I know what I said, but I think maybe Dannie's right."

"Of course, I'm right. I'm always right," she turns back to me. "And you need to pull your head out of you're a –"

"Uh, children are present," Walker interrupts her.

"Just pull your head out! You guys crossed the professional line long ago. You've spent almost every single day with her for the last two months! And you've been moping for the last three days like you have some gloomy cloud hanging over you and we all know why."

I do know why. I could pretend I don't, but I think that would make me look even more like an idiot. We all know it has everything to do with the forceful blonde just outside the door that I desperately want to see again.

But it's not that easy.

"I don't think I can do this," I whisper, barely audible. Ellie's face instantly changes.

"Wyatt, you deserve to be happy. Stop living in the past." She steps closer and grabs my face, forcing me to look her in the eye. "People can change. You've proven that time and time again. You're not the same person you were five years ago."

She always could read me so easily. And she's just gotten better at it over the years. All the things I've tried to cover with sarcasm and denial boil to the surface and she sees them all.

I gently pull her hands from my face. "I don't deserve her, Ellie."

How could I deserve something that beautiful and fragile when I break everything I touch?

"You're a *good* person and you deserve good things. Stop telling yourself you don't."

"She's right, you know," Walker says behind her. "And I've now had to admit that twice in ten minutes, so you owe me."

I chuckle half-heartedly.

"Do you remember that first summer," Ellie says with a small smile. "After you came back and stayed with us for a couple weeks?"

My eyebrows bunch, unsure where this is going. "Yeah."

"Do you remember what you said to me that first night?"

I do remember. It was an awkward night at first. Neither one of us knew what to say to each other. We were such different people than the ones we used to know. Lincoln was sleeping on my chest and I didn't want to move. I would've stayed like that all night so I wouldn't disturb him.

We'd been sitting in silence for what felt like hours when I finally decided to speak.

"You're so different."

"Yeah, well, people change, Wyatt," she replied almost impatiently.

"I know."

The silence resurfaced for a minute before she asked, "Different how?"

I shrugged and Lincoln stirred. I waited until he calmed down again before I replied. "I mean, you're still the same, just...stronger."

She looked at me for the longest time, but didn't say a word.

"What changed?" I finally asked.

"I did," she said simply. "And I found Walker."

I look at her now, her child standing next to her and another on the way and she's somehow stronger still.

"You're different, too. You've changed, Wyatt. Stop punishing yourself for the past. Let yourself have a future."

Fear is a strange thing. People talk about fear often, usually about things like spiders, clowns, or snakes. Things we can see, touch, and feel. No one prepares you for this kind of fear. The kind that constantly tells you that you're not good enough. The kind that reminds you no one could ever love you. The kind that promises you that you'll always fail no matter how hard you try.

But there's power in facing your fears. Just like Ellie did by leaving me. By trusting Walker. She was always brave, but she never really saw it the way others did. She just never saw herself clearly.

Until Walker.

I look at her and Walker, his arm around her shoulders and hers around his waist. I see the family they've created, the *life* they have. I think of all the times I've found myself coming over just to feel like I'm a part of something.

But I can't keep living vicariously through them and all that could've been; throwing myself pity parties everyday when I go home to an empty house and reliving all the bad choices that got me there.

At some point I have to move forward just like Ellie said. I have to believe in hope. In that hope I see in Ellie's eyes ever since Walker walked into her life.

The same glimmer of hope I've felt ever since Lucy showed up in those red heels with her blue binder.

I squeeze Ellie's arm and kiss her forehead before bolting through the dining room calling over my shoulders, "Thanks, Ellie."

I pray she's still outside as I burst through the front door and I catch her just as she's climbing into the driver's seat of the truck.

"Wait!" I call and she turns toward me, eyes wide.

"Get dinner with me."

It comes out considerably more aggressive than I expected and sounds more like a demand than a question.

Her eyes widen as she drops back to the ground. "Excuse me?"

"Sorry," I say much calmer this time. "That wasn't exactly how I planned on doing that."

"Doing what?"

"Asking you out."

Her eyes get even wider. "You're asking me out?"

"Yes."

"Oh," she pipes. "Well, don't let me stop you. Please, continue." She stands straighter, clasping her hands in front of her. Smiling softly.

I clear my throat and take a step closer. She doesn't move so I take another.

"What are you doing tomorrow night? Now that the project's complete."

"Well, my usual evenings consist of watching nineteen-fifties sitcoms and eating various forms of cheese crackers. Why do you ask?" She bats her eyelashes at me dramatically.

She's messing with me. And it makes all of this suddenly so much easier.

"I was wondering if you'd want to get dinner with me tomorrow night?"

"Are you asking me on a date?" She drops her hand on her chest and pops her mouth open in mock surprise.

I chuckle. "Yes, Lucy, I'm asking you on a date."

"I don't know, I was told never to mix business with pleasure."

"Well, the project's done. We're not working together anymore."

"That's true, but I'm still not sure," she teases. "It's a risky little game."

She's enjoying this too much and thinks she's in control.

It's time to step up my game.

I close all space between us, and drop my hand on her hip, giving it a light squeeze as I dip down and whisper in her ear, "Have dinner with me, Lucy."

chapter twenty-three
lucy

This is so unfair.

His voice is rough and his breath is tickling my ear.

He takes another step getting somehow closer, which I wouldn't have thought possible, until his full body is pressed against mine and he whispers in my ear again, "Have dinner with me, Lucy."

How could I even say no?

In the back of my mind, I think that if any other man grabbed me this way and asked me on a date I would shove him back so quickly and find his groin with my knee, but Wyatt is different.

Isn't that the point?

I want to say yes, I want to shout it! But I can't find my voice so I simply nod once.

I can feel his smile on my ear and his lips barely graze my cheek as he pulls back.

"Can you meet me here at six tomorrow?"

I nod again, my voice still somewhere far, far away. I wonder if I'll ever get it back.

"I'll see you tomorrow, Lucy."

He doesn't wait for a response. He turns his back to me and walks back through the front door of the restaurant much more confident than when he burst out of it and demanded dinner in a rushed slur of words I wasn't even sure I'd heard right. I'm still standing in the same spot, mouth agape as I see Walker and his wife sneak out the back door and drive away.

Wyatt Reed just asked me out.

"Jenny!" I yell as I burst into the apartment.

"What is with all the yelling these days?" she demands, stepping out of the kitchen, a bowl of cereal in her hands. Her hair is in a messy bun and she's in sweats and I'm grateful she's in for the night because this is going to take a while. "Remember the good ole' days when you announced yourself at a perfectly reasonable decibel?"

"He asked me out."

She drops her bowl of cereal on the counter, milk flying everywhere. "Tell me everything."

I proceed to do just that, giving her every tiny detail all the way down to his hand placements and the husky timbre of his voice in my ear. The tickle of his stubble on my face when he asked me out.

"Heaven help me, I need a man," she droops against the back of the couch.

"You're blushing."

"Stop," she holds her hand up and closes her eyes. "I'm daydreaming."

"Not about my man, you're not."

She opens her eyes and smirks. "So, he's your man now?"

"No, he's just..." I stammer.

"Come on, Luce, you've been talking about him nonstop for weeks. All I've heard is Wyatt this and Wyatt that. 'Did you know Wyatt went to NYU?' 'Did you know Wyatt is from Virginia?' 'Did you know Wyatt is beautiful and so sexy and I'm so in love with him I might die if he doesn't grab me and have his way with me?'"

"Okay, I never said that last one."

"You may as well have. You have been talking about him all day, every day. If I wasn't so happy for you I'd have told you to shut up weeks ago."

"Okay, I will admit that I've mentioned him a time or two, but – "

"A time or two? Don't play dumb. He's like your new best friend. Second best friend, of course, because no one could ever replace me."

"Of course, Jenny. You'll always be number one."

Jenny has been my best friend forever. I don't know life without her. She's the person I've always called in good or bad times. The one who has stood by me through every bad date, failed class and news-worthy event in my life.

I talk to her about everything.

But I've never talked to anyone the way I talk to Wyatt. Not even Jenny. There's a peace I find in conversations with him. Maybe it's the way he listens so intently, remembering every word. I never have to repeat myself or ask if he's listening. He doesn't tell me to talk slower or softer. He just listens. He's confident in the best way, but still knows the importance of humility. He sells himself short sometimes, but not to the degree that he's a pushover. His voice softens when he talks about his family, especially Lincoln. He laughs at himself often and never fails to ask about my day.

He's the easiest person to talk to; to be around. I'm comfortable with him in ways I've never been comfortable with anyone.

"How did this happen?" I murmur. "I didn't even know he existed two months ago. How can I feel so connected to someone I barely know?"

Jenny shrugs. "I don't know. I think maybe people come into our lives at a certain time for a reason. Maybe he isn't the love of your life, but this could be a really good experience. Take a chance. On yourself, *for* yourself."

"What if it's not good? What if without the topic of the restaurant renovations we have nothing to talk about?"

"When, in the last two months, did you even talk about the renovations except when necessary?"

"Hardly at all," I admit.

"It's not going to be any different than all the other times you guys have talked for hours on end, okay? It's going to be great."

"Thanks Jenny. You're the best pretend sister ever."

"I know! Now can we pick out something for you to wear?"

I chuckle. "Yes!"

"Great," she says grabbing my arm and pulling me toward her room. "But we're gonna have to do that in my closet, because I can guarantee you don't have anything appropriate for the date of the century."

chapter twenty-four
wyatt

Whose grand idea was it to cook dinner?

Oh, right, mine.

I regret that decision as soon as I step into the restaurant's dark, empty kitchen. I'm rarely in here and it feels much bigger than normal. Only the emergency lights are on, making it eerily dark.

I flip the switch to turn on the fluorescents, take a deep breath and get to work before I chicken out.

I asked Walker to send me the easiest recipe he could think of that didn't feel cheap. He sent me his recipe for chicken alfredo. Well, it's really our mom's alfredo, but Walker's adjusted it over the years. It's the best alfredo I've ever had in my life and the recipe didn't look too complicated. I'm not exactly a wiz in the kitchen. I make a mean grilled cheese sandwich, but that's the limit of my abilities.

Yesterday, when I asked her to meet me here, it was because I'd asked her rather abruptly and I didn't have any time to make a plan. Figured we could meet here and then I'd drive her somewhere nice. But that felt too formal somehow. I considered a million different options, but this seemed the most comfortable. We knew each other in this space. It's where we've spent all of our time. I think Lucy will be most comfortable here.

The recipe isn't complicated, just as Walker promised. My roux is the biggest trial, not getting it thick enough and then getting it too thick and having a hard time getting the chunks out. Luckily it comes together after some internet searches where I learned how to spell roux. I'm just putting our full plates on the table when there's a knock on the back door at exactly six o'clock.

I wipe my hands on a damp towel and smooth my hair.

My heart is racing a million miles a minute and my hands are getting clammy, but when I walk through the kitchen to find her peeking through the small window, grin wide and waving at me, all that anxiety disappears.

"I hear you did some renovations," she smiles, peeking her head in the second I open the door. "It looks good. I must get the name of your contractor."

I chuckle as she practically skips in, and I shut the door behind her.

"Funny, I don't remember changes made to the ki – "

My words fall short when I turn back and catch full sight of her for the first time.

She's wearing a soft blue dress that wraps tightly around her waist. She has a sleeve all the way to her wrist on the left side, but her right arm and shoulder are bare. The dress barely brushes the top of her knees. She's wearing heels, but they aren't very tall, and her hands are clasped in front of her. Her hair is wavy today and her lips lightly glossy. I save her eyes for last, knowing I'll get lost in them and wouldn't want to miss the rest.

Her eyes are bluer somehow, the dress making them shimmer.

"You look beautiful."

She blushes beet red but doesn't try to hide it. She wears it proudly as she says, "Thank you. You're not looking too bad yourself." She takes me in from head to toe, eyes lingering on the green sweater I chose for a reason. It hugs my chest just right and makes my pecs look way more muscular than they are. Something she clearly notices; the look in her eye has me involuntarily puffing my chest out. Finally, she moves up to my eyes and higher. "Did you blow dry your hair?"

I run a hand over the strands I had to comb seventy times to get it this smooth. "No, but I did brush it."

She looks at me in disbelief. "Do you not always brush your hair?"

I shrug. "Not really. I usually just run my fingers through it after I wash it."

She laughs once. "So, it is naturally flowy, then?"

I raise a furrowed brow. "Flowy?"

"Never mind," she smiles. "What's for dinner?"

I hold my hand out for her. "Follow me."

She slips her small fingers around mine and I lead her through the kitchen and into the dining room.

I got here two hours early to set everything up. I moved all the tables against the walls and left one small, two-person table in the center of the room. I dimmed the main lights, the majority of light coming from the strings around the perimeter of the room and the few candles I lit.

I barely slept last night planning it all out and woke up early to hit the grocery store to get all the ingredients, but seeing the awestruck look on her face makes every single minute worth it.

"You finally going to take that picture?"

Her voice breaks my tracne and I realize I've been staring.

"Did you finally bring that camera?"

She giggles, her skirt swaying side to side.

"You just look so different," I explain as I lead her to the table, pulling out her chair.

She tosses her hair back dramatically, though it's so short it barely moves. "I clean up pretty good, I know."

"Well, yes," I take the seat across from her. "But I meant, I've never seen you without that blue binder in your hand. Wasn't sure if it was even you when I opened the door."

"Hey, don't diss the binder. That thing made all of this," she gestures to the room around us, "possible."

"It really is incredible, Lucy. You did great."

"My crew did great. And you!" she exclaims, looking down at the table for the first time. "I love alfredo, this looks delicious."

She takes a bite and a small moan escapes and I feel my stomach jump in a way it hasn't in years.

"This is the best alfredo I've ever had! I thought Walker was the chef."

"Well, I've learned a thing or two over the years."

"Clearly," she says through a mouthful. "This is amazing."

"Thanks, it's an easy recipe," I admit. "I haven't actually learned that much."

She giggles as we fall into an easy banter over dinner. To think I worried we wouldn't have anything to talk about or that it would be awkward without the renovations to discuss. I came up with different conversation points in my mind that I could bring up whenever conversation lagged, but I haven't had to use it once. There's no topic we don't touch from our favorite food to our favorite places we've visited.

"Honestly, I haven't really been many places, but I would say my favorite is probably North Carolina," she says. "It's just so beautiful and the water is blue and the people are so nice. I love it."

"Have you been out west at all?"

She shakes her head. "My cousin Jenny and I want to go to L.A. for Christmas this year, but I don't know if our mothers would appreciate us ditching the family for California on Christmas Day."

"I know your family all live in state, but how close?"

She laughs once. "Too close. My brothers all live within about two hours of my parents' house and I obviously work in the family business. I have an apartment with Jenny that's around the corner from my parents." She leans back in her chair, half her plate still full. I might've over done it.

"That's kind of nice, though. I wish Winnie lived closer."

"They're in Chicago, right?"

I nod. "Temporarily. He's there for his PhD, but she's hoping to move back to Virginia to be closer to my mom."

"Did you grow up in Virginia?"

I nod. "Yeah. I moved out for NYU and then stayed in the city. Until I moved here three years ago."

"I've always wanted to go to Virginia."

"Maybe I can take you there sometime."

Her smile spreads wider and another blush brightens her cheeks. "That would be nice."

The conversation shifts again with ease, like we've known each other our whole lives and we've just been waiting to share the latest with each other.

When her plate finally clears, she leans back in her chair, her hand resting on her stomach. "That was too good. You might have to talk to Walker about switching positions."

I chuckle. "Yeah, we'll strictly sell alfredo and my specialty: grilled cheese."

"Oh, grilled cheese is the best. You can put that on the menu next time."

The promise of a next time does strange things to my chest as I take our plates and gather the silverware. "Now it's time for dessert."

I hurry into the kitchen to drop the dirty dishes in the sink to worry about later and bring out two strawberry cupcakes.

"I have to admit," I start as I enter the dining room. "Walker made the cupcakes. It's a family recipe and – "

I stop short when I find the table empty.

"Lucy?" I call out, leaving the cupcakes on the table.

"Over here."

I turn to the sound of her voice and find her in the south side of the building standing in the small circular alcove that was part of the expansion. The nook as she calls it.

"You never ordered the cushions, did you?" she asks, eyeing the bare wood bench surrounding the window.

I chuckle. "Never quite got around to it, no. I told you to just pick whatever you thought looked best."

"It's not my restaurant."

"It was all your design, though."

She blushes again and turns her attention to the expansion. "It's still so crazy," she marvels. "Seeing my design like this." She looks around the room, moving slowly as she takes it all in.

"You did an incredible job, Lucy."

"Thank you," she blushes, and I don't think I've ever seen anything so beautiful.

Our gazes hold for a long minute and I'm about to close the distance between us when she asks, "Can I ask you a question?"

"Of course."

"That rough patch you mentioned..."

She trails off as if she expects me to know the rest of the question, but I'm not sure where she's going with this.

"Does that have anything to do with why you bought sparkling cider for tonight instead of wine?"

I nod.

"Do you not drink?"

"No."

"Why?"

"Because I used to drink too much."

"I guessed that," she says simply with nothing but curiosity in her tone. "What changed?"

"Lincoln."

She smiles warmly. "Kids have a tendency to do that."

"Yeah, they do."

"Have you ever thought about having kids of your own?"

Her bright eyes and eager smile bring that lump back in my throat a little. Everything up until now has been so easy. I haven't once questioned sharing anything with her, but this is different. How would she look at me if she knew the truth?

I shift awkwardly on my feet, tucking my hands in my pockets. "Um, yeah, I have."

"Do you want a big family?"

I shrug.

"But you want kids?"

"I don't know." It's probably the most honest thing I've said all night.

"Sorry," she says with a tuck of her hair behind her ears. "This is probably too personal for a first date."

"It's not like we're strangers, Lucy. This isn't an average first date."

"No, it's not," she blushes.

She pushes her glasses up the bridge of her nose and I don't think, I just move. My hand reaches for hers that's still on her glasses and I wrap my hand around her wrist, pulling her close to me, as I wrap my other arm around her waist.

She sucks in a quick breath and her mouth opens slightly. I'm just leaning in when a hand on my chest stops me.

"I should tell you," she whispers, "I don't kiss on the first date."

"Then call it a business meeting," I whisper, leaning closer.

She giggles breathlessly. "Funny enough, I don't usually kiss in business meetings either."

"Usually?" I squeeze her hips.

"Never. I *never* kiss in business meetings," she breaths.

"That's too bad." I brush my lips against her cheek. "What about second dates? Do you kiss on second dates?"

She tilts her head back to catch my eyes, forcing her body into mine. I can feel her breath coming quicker, her chest just barely brushing my stomach with each breath. "Maybe. Depends on how good the second date is."

I squeeze her hips again and leave a soft kiss on her temple before I take a small step back. My hands remain resting on her waist – not wanting to let go of her, but I leave enough space for both of us to think clearly. The look of disappointment on her face tells me everything I need to know.

"It's going to be the best second date of your life, sweetheart."

She laughs once, her breathing still uneven. "You're different, Wyatt Reed."

"Funny. I was going to say the same thing about you, Lucy Snow."

"Different in a good way?"

I tuck her hair behind her ear. "In the best way."

chapter twenty-five
lucy

"I can't believe he didn't kiss you!" Jenny exclaims as we sit on the couch eating every candy we could find in the pantry.

We didn't waste any time after I got home. Jenny was already in the living room having raided the pantry and I grabbed the ice cream out of the freezer, kicked my shoes into my room and plopped onto the couch to give her every excruciating detail.

"I thought it was sweet. I told him I don't kiss on the first date."

Honestly, I was a little disappointed that he didn't kiss me at first, but he was respecting my wishes. A lot of guys would've kissed me even if I said no, thinking it would change my mind or that they knew what I wanted better than

I did. I told him one time that I didn't kiss on the first date and he respected that.

And after our almost kiss in the bathroom, I wanted to make sure we took things slow and steady. There's been this tension between us since day one. Almost like some crazy gravitational pull always trying to connect us, but I've done that before. I've made out with guys on a first date and then never heard from them again. I've kissed boys who felt like they could be 'the one,' only to have my heart broken. I'm not doing that this time. I'm not getting caught up in emotions. I don't want to rush anything or force anything with Wyatt. I want to take my time with him.

When I left, he walked me to my car, opened the door for me and tenderly kissed my cheek, assuring me he would call tomorrow.

It was the best first date of my life.

"Yeah, but that's only because you've had crappy first dates in the last five years. Who would want to kiss any of those drips? This is Wyatt Reed."

"You can just call him Wyatt, you know."

"Yeah, but Wyatt Reed just sounds more manly. Sexier." She pauses for a moment, looking far off.

"Are you daydreaming again?"

Her eyes go wide. "Maybe."

I chuck a sour candy at her.

"Sorry! Are you going to kiss him next time?"

"I don't know."

"Well, if *you* don't kiss him, honey, I will."

I wake up in the most uncomfortable position. Folded in ways I didn't even know I could bend. Though the ache in my neck and back tell me I can't, in fact, bend that way. I open my eyes just enough to find Jenny beside me on the couch snoring softly.

I fish around until I find my phone on the floor to check the time. 6am. I groan as I sit up and wipe the sleep from my eyes. It's not until I glance at my phone a second time that I notice an unread message that came through an hour ago. Who wakes up that early on a Sunday?

Wyatt: When can I see you again?

I respond so quickly there's a million typos and I have to read it five times before I even realize what I said.

Lucy: Is tight tii desolate!

I groan even louder as I throw my head back on the couch. Can I ever stop humiliating myself?

Jenny always says you should never double text a guy, but what else am I supposed to do? I check to make sure she's still asleep and text him again.

Lucy: Sorry. Sleep deprived. That was supposed to say - is tonight too desperate?

Wyatt: Tonight isn't desperate enough.

The smile that takes over my face is embarrassing.

The texting continues throughout the day.

As I pull into the parking lot at work I get:

Wyatt: I dreamed about you last night.

Lucy: Oh, do tell.

Wyatt: It was our first date, except this time you let me kiss you.

Lucy: Most definitely a dream then.

Wyatt: True. Cause if we had kissed last night, I never would've been able to fall asleep from replaying it over and over...

Later, after lunch I text him:

Lucy: Any dress code for tonight?

Wyatt: Dress comfortably.

Lucy: You're such a man. That doesn't help me. Comfortable could be a dress and heels or the oversized sweatshirt and shorts I sleep in.

Wyatt: Definitely the sleep shorts.

Lucy: Wyatt...

Wyatt: Closed toed shoes and a jacket. I think it's going to snow again tonight.

Wyatt: Can I pick you up? If you'd rather meet at the location, I understand.

Lucy: Pick me up.

I'm just sending him my address when I hear, "Who's the guy?"

I practically jump out of my chair to find my brother looming over my shoulder.

"Landon! You scared the crap out of me. What are you doing here?"

He stuffs his hands in his pockets, unfazed. "I work here."

"Could've fooled me," I mumble as I straighten the papers on my desk.

"Very funny. For real, though. I'm officially back from paternity leave."

I look up to his wide grin. "Wait, really? Is Samantha okay with this?"

"Not even a little," he chuckles, "but life goes on and we need some money. I don't think dad's going to keep paying me without work for much longer."

"Fair enough. Here you go." I drop my blue binder in his unprepared hands and he fumbles, barely catching it before everything falls out. "That is your bible. Treat it as such."

"Where are you going?" he asks, checking his watch as I slip my purse on my shoulder and grab my keys off the hook by the door. "It's only three o'clock."

"I'm taking some time off."

He smiles. "So there *is* a guy."

"Says who?"

"Says you. Never in all my life have I seen you take time off. You did homework until all hours of the night in high school. You took summer classes in college, and you've never used any PTO. I would know; I do payroll."

He folds his arms over his chest. "So, who's the guy?"

"Maybe Jenny and I are having a girls' night."

He raises a disbelieving brow.

"Ugh, fine," I drop my hands at my sides. "If you must know, nosy, I have a date tonight and I don't have anything to wear so I'm going to stop at the store on my way home."

"Who's the lucky guy?"

"None of your business."

"Yeah right. Where did you meet him?"

I can feel the heat on my cheeks, and I try to hide it as I look for nothing in particular in my purse.

"Did you meet him at work?" he presses.

That has my head shooting up. "What makes you say that?"

"You do nothing but work. Where else would you meet a man?"

I narrow my eyes and he narrows his right back. "Yes. I mean, no. Well, not technically." Does it count as meeting at the foot truck if we didn't actually introduce ourselves. I didn't even know his name yet. He was just the sexy stranger.

"And you don't think this is a conflict of interest?"

"No, the project's done."

"Don't tell me you actually waited until the project was done?"

"What's wrong with that? You just said it was a conflict of interest."

"No, I was surprised *you* didn't think it was a conflict of interest, but of course you did." He chuckles.

"Look, I'm not really ready for anyone to know about this. Can you please just keep this to yourself for now?"

"My lips are sealed." He pretends to zip his lips and throw away the key. "Though you might need to tell Jared. He's the one who told me you had eyes for someone at work."

"Don't say 'had eyes,' you sound like an old man. And how would Jared even know?"

"He drove by the restaurant last night and saw your car. He thought the job was done, so he called me. And funny enough, when I checked the system, it was marked complete."

"So now you all are spying on me?"

"No one was spying, but you're our little sister. We want to know what you're doing until all hours of the night at a closed restaurant with a man we don't know."

"Ugh, you guys are impossible."

"Is he good enough for you?"

I smile softly. "You don't need to go all big-brotherly on me, Landon. I can take care of myself."

"I know you can. But that can get kind of exhausting sometimes. So just know I'm here if you need me to kick him in the nuts."

I roll my eyes. "Thanks Landon." I point to the binder he's holding too carelessly. "And I'm serious about that binder. *Bible.* Don't lose it, break it, drop it, forget it, nothing! It stays tied to you. *Glued.* Actually, we have some glue..." I look around the office.

"I get it, I get it. Guard it with my life."

"That's what I'm talking about."

With that I turn on my heel and head to the mall.

I'm unlucky at any of the department stores, which means I have to raid Jenny's closet when I get home. She's out with some friends from work for the night, so I have free rein, but everything in her closet is too fancy.

I meander back to my closet and settle on a pair of jeans and a square neck blouse. It's simple, but still looks like I made effort. My hair is straight as per usual, one side behind my ear. I throw on a little tinted lip gloss and examine myself in the mirror.

The skinny jeans are a bit baggy and I'm pretty sure outdated, but they're the only jeans I have that aren't work pants. They're a so big they make me look like I have elephant knees. I've been on my feet so much lately, I think I've lost a few pounds without realizing.

The shirt fits nicely and accentuates the small bust I have, making it look a little more appealing than the poor mosquito bites they are.

It's not great, but it's good. We shouldn't be putting so much importance on our attire anyway. If Wyatt likes me, what does it matter what I wear? Who cares if my jeans are too small or too tight. He should like me for me, not my jean size.

I'm just picking out shoes when my doorbell rings at exactly seven o'clock and I practically run to answer it.

"Hi," I chime as I open the door.

He's dressed simply, in a blue sweater and jeans. I'm pretty sure he has this sweater in every other color because

I've seen it before. And he's in the same black jeans he must have seven pairs. It's all he wears. His hair is combed more than I've ever seen and I can smell a slight hint of cologne.

"Hi, Lucy." A simple greeting like this shouldn't have my heart racing, but here we are.

"I like your sweater," I say, admiring said sweater. Well, admiring the pecs more than anything, but no one can prove that. "Is it the same one you wore yesterday?"

He chuckles. "Yeah, I have it in eight colors."

"It's a good sweater," I mumble, my gaze focused on the sweater. Only the sweater.

"You look incredible, as always." He smiles that crooked grin that should be illegal. "Are you ready to go?"

"I just have to grab my shoes, you can come in."

I turn away, but am stopped by his hand on my arm, pulling me toward him. His arm wraps around my waist while the other rests on my jaw.

"This is our second date," he whispers, his voice raspy, as he drops his forehead to mine.

"It is," I barely manage to say.

"Does that mean I can kiss you now?"

I respond the only way I know how, my voice long lost once again. I grab his face in my hands and crush my lips to his. He responds quickly, his lips prying mine open as he sighs into my mouth.

His hands gripping my waist, his lips moving down my neck, the feel of his hair in my hands, the small moan he makes when I tighten my grip at the nap of his neck. This is the kind of kiss people dream about.

This is the kind of kiss people write books about.

I pull away first, out of breath and overwhelmed.

"You were right," I mumble, catching my breath.

"About what?" he pulls back just enough to catch my eye.

"This is the best second date of my entire life."

He chuckles. "It hasn't even started yet."

"Right. Can we just skip to the part where we come back here and kiss on the porch?"

His hands tighten on my hips. "Oh, we'll get to that part, I promise."

He releases me and gives me a playful shove. "Get your shoes, we have a reservation."

"I'm intrigued. Where?"

"You'll see when we get there."

I slip into my white sneakers and grab my purse that's hanging behind the front door. "I don't like surprises."

"You'll like this surprise."

I come up with a million different places he could be taking me as we drive through town. With every turn he takes, I guess, each time coming up wrong. It's not until we pull into a parking lot I'm unfamiliar with that he tells me what we're doing.

"I told you closed-toed shoes for a reason," he starts as we gets out of the car. "I only heard about this place a couple weeks ago. I got lucky that they had a class tonight. Even luckier that they had empty spots. Well, only one empty spot. I had to do some convincing to let them allow both of us in. We're gonna have to share a project."

"Project?" I question.

He takes my hand in his and leads me through the front door.

There are long high tables set up around a huge, open room. Each table filled with various pieces of wood, safety glasses and sanders.

"It's a woodshop class. Figured I should get better at my sanding," he winks.

Once. I told him one time that I loved sanding. It was a playful conversation, the second time we ever spoke to each other. I mentioned it one time and he remembered.

I could cry.

I raise up on my tip toes to press a kiss to his lips.

"This is without a doubt, the most incredible second, first, any date I've ever been on in my life."

He tilts his head just right, that his gaze goes through his eyelashes. "So, I definitely get a kiss goodnight?"

"Without a doubt."

The class starts then and we're instructed on the basics before we can start analyzing the wood options on the table.

"So," Wyatt starts. "What is it about wood-working that you so much?"

"A lot of things," I reply as I put on my safety glasses and get to work. "I like working with my hands, I always have. I've never been one to sit still. I was always doodling when I was a kid on anything and everything I could find. My mom got upset with me one time because I drew, with permanent marker, on her tablecloth." I laugh at the memory. "I just liked creating things and I needed an outlet. So, my dad started taking me to work with him. He let me help out when I could. I just fell in love with construction, building in general. I mean, you're literally creating something from nothing. Someone can drive by an empty piece of land and think, 'that could be beautiful.' My dad had some pretty big projects when I was a kid and I saw that exact thing happen over and over again."

"Hence architecture," he adds.

"Yup! Like I said, I always loved drawing, doodling around. And when I fell in love with construction, it all just kind of came together. My dad was pretty good friends with one of the architects in the city and asked if I could intern when I was a senior in high school. After that, I went to NYU and I loved it."

"But you're a contractor? Why? If you want to be an architect why don't you do that?"

My hands pause. We were doing so well and then he had to go and ask the hard questions.

I keep my head down as I respond. "I love construction and I love working for my dad. It's not that I don't want to stay there, it's just not *all* I want. I want to be more than that."

"Then why don't you?"

Jenny's asked me this question so many times. The answer never actually spoken aloud, the truth too hard to speak allowed.

Wyatt looks at me with an intense curiosity, a genuine interest in my answer, waiting for me to say the words I've never been able to speak before.

"I think I'm afraid."

"You're afraid? That surprises me."

"Everyone is afraid of something."

He pulls the safety glasses from my face and steps closer. "Why are you afraid?"

"Because what if I fail? I'm really good at what I do. I'm good at networking and talking to people. I am really good at project management and keeping everything in order. And I think I'm good at all of that because I have my dad's last name. People don't respect me because I'm a hard worker and they value what I can do. They respect me because they respect Nick Snow."

As the words come out I feel a physical weight lift from my shoulders. Getting it out in the open feels freeing in a way I didn't know was possible.

Wyatt smiles softly and traces a finger down my cheek.

"I've said it before, but I'll say it again. You're a force, Lucy Snow. People respect you because you earn that respect with the way you show up and do what needs to be done. With the way you respect others and demand that same respect back. You're your own person. You're incredible because of what *you* have accomplished. Don't give your father credit for your success. Own it."

He wipes a tear that I didn't realize had fallen and I chuckle breathlessly, taking a step back. "Sorry, I'm such a baby. That was a very nice speech."

"It wasn't a speech, Lucy," he whispers.

I catch his eye, getting lost in the darkness that somehow feels so bright.

"Thanks, Wyatt," I whisper.

"So, what do you want to do? If you could do anything in the world, what would it be?"

"Both," I wipe the tears from my face. "I still want to work for my dad. One day the business could be mine and Landon's. But I'd like to have my designs in front of the clients, too. I understand they might not always choose it, but it would be nice to be able to do both. I don't want to have to choose between my dad and my dreams. They can both be the same."

"Have you talked to him about it?"

"Not really. The restaurant was actually kind of a test project that he offered me. He told me if I could handle this account then we'd talk about my future with the business, but...we haven't talked about any of it yet."

"Why do you think that is?" he asks.

I shrug. "I don't know. Jenny will say it's because we suck at communicating. She's not wrong, but it's more than that. I'm scarred to put it all out there and my dad can be a bit stubborn." I groan at myself. "I sound like such a spoiled brat. My dad is incredible and has done so much for me. I don't want you to think he's not."

"I don't think that," he assures me. "But it's okay to fight for yourself. It doesn't mean that you respect or love him any less."

"You sound like my cousin Jenny."

"Well, she sounds very smart."

"I'll tell her you said that. You'll be on her good side for the rest of time."

He chuckles and holds the safety glasses out to me. "Should we get back to work?"

"Yes, but this time," I grab the safety glasses and slide them onto his nose. "You do the sanding."

chapter twenty-six
wyatt

One week.

Seven days.

That's all it takes for your life to change.

Lucy and I have spent every night together for the last seven days. Each day more exciting than the last. Each night getting harder to say goodbye on that damn porch.

The restaurant reopening has been pretty smooth. Walker said the kitchen was a bit hectic with more people in the dining room and posted another job opening, but he's handled the extra load well. Apart from having to bus a few tables the first two nights back and hiring a new employee, my work load has been consistent. Even still, I'm grateful when Saturday comes.

I didn't wait long after dropping Lucy off on Friday night to text her about her Saturday plans.

Wyatt: What are you doing tomorrow?

Lucy: Already want to see me again?

Wyatt: Am I sounding too desperate now?

Lucy: Not desperate enough.

Lucy: But I have one request?

Wyatt: Anything

Lucy: I get to pick where we go. There's this little café not far from my house that's so good. They have amazing bagel breakfast sandwiches!!

Wyatt: Sounds good to me. What time do you want me to pick you up?

Lucy: Eight?

Wyatt: I'll see you then, beautiful.

I picked her up right on time and drove us the short mile to the café.

"Their coffee is good. I've heard. I don't drink it, but –"

"You don't drink coffee?" I ask, opening the door for her.

"Nope. Never in my life."

"Why not?"

She shrugs as we get in the line. "Honestly, I hate the smell. My dad drinks it, but my mom hates it. We never had it in the house, but my dad has a machine in his office. I always thought it smelled funny. Also, I just don't like flavored drinks. I drink water and not much else. If I'm feeling really fancy, I'll grab a sparkling water or a cider, but that's only for special occasions."

"You don't like flavored beverages? Haven't heard that one before."

"Why do I want to drink, like, strawberry lemonade while I'm eating a burger? If I put strawberries on my burger people would think I was insane!"

I laugh at the analogy. "You make a very valid point, Miss Snow."

She orders a simple egg sandwich with cheese as we step up to the counter and I order the spinach omelet on an asiago bagel.

"Oh, here," Lucy chimes as I pull my wallet out. "I'll pay for this one. It was my idea."

"No, I got it, don't worry about it."

"Wyatt," she puts her hands on her hips and she looks like my contractor again. "We've been out five times this week and you've paid for each one. Let me buy you a six-dollar bagel."

I chuckle as I slide my wallet back in my pocket. "Yes, ma'am."

"That's right." She pays with cash, and we wait in the corner for only a few minutes when they call our name.

"Do you mind eating outside? It's nice outside and it's kind of crowded in here." She looks around at the full tables.

"Sure."

She makes her way outside, straight to the corner table closest to the street, like she's done this before.

"Is this your usual table?" I ask, taking a seat next to her.

She nods, mouth full of food.

I chuckle at her cheek protruding around the bagel and wipe the corner of her mouth with my napkin.

"Thanks," she mumbles, eyes wide.

I dig into my own sandwich and it doesn't take long to realize she was right.

"Wow," I say around a mouthful. "This is delicious."

"I told you! My parents used to bring us here every Saturday morning. When I was a kid, you got a free chocolate milk with any kids meal on Saturday mornings. I don't know if they still do that, but we loved it!"

"So is it the bagel or the nostalgia that makes you love it so much?"

"Both."

"Speaking of your parents..."

She avoids my eyes. "I haven't talked to my dad yet. Honestly, it's been really busy trying to get everything closed out with end of year coming and we have to really be caught up before the holidays. But I have family night with them on Monday and I'm going to ask, I promise."

I put my hand on her arm to stop her rambling. "It's okay to be nervous. This is your whole career, but don't be so afraid you don't ask."

"I know, I know, but I don't want to talk about that right now." She takes another bite of her bagel. "What about you? Any nostalgic places you like to go when you go home?"

I'm tempted to push the issue more with her dad, but I don't want to step on toes. It's her relationship, not mine. I just want to know she's doing what's best for her, not what everyone else thinks is best.

I open my mouth to say just that, but think better of it when she shoots me a glare like she knows exactly what words are on the tip of my tongue.

"Not a place, no, but my mom makes really good chocolate chip cookies. She would always make them for us for our birthday and make like a little tower out of them because she couldn't make cakes."

"That's cute. Does she share the recipe?"

"She used to, but we use it at the restaurant now. Actually, a lot of our greatest recipes are my mom's that Walker's adjusted over the years."

"I saw you guys had a giant chocolate chip cookie a la mode on the menu. It sounded amazing!"

"Well, we'll have to get one next week."

"Sounds good," she shivers as she speaks and drops her bagel to rub her arms.

"You're cold," I say.

"I'm fine," she waves me off. "I just forgot my sweater when we left. It's on my couch."

"You can have mine." I drop my bagel on the table and wipe my hands on my napkin.

She chuckles. "Come on, Wyatt, it's not that bad. I'll be fine."

I pull my favorite sweater over my head leaving me in nothing but a white t-shirt as I hold the sweater out to her. I'll be freezing, but I'll live. Her eyes widen and her lips part slightly. I'm not a religious person, but if anything will make me believe in heaven it's her looking at me like that.

"I can't take your sweater, Wyatt. Then you'll be cold."

I shrug one shoulder. "Then I'll be cold."

"Wyatt."

"Lucy."

She stares at me for a beat before she carefully takes the sweater from my hand, eyes never leaving mine. I watch, completely transfixed, as she pushes her arms through the sleeves and pulls it over her head. It's big on her, of course. She has to roll the sleeves twice to prevent them from covering her hands. I've seen women in skintight black dresses, short shorts, miniskirts, the skimpiest outfits, with skin exposed for all to see and nothing has ever been sexier than Lucy Snow, completely covered, in *my* green sweater.

Oh boy, am I in trouble.

chapter twenty-seven
lucy

I'm pretty sure I'm dating Wyatt Reed.

Okay, I'm totally dating Wyatt Reed.

That was unexpected.

It's been two weeks of snowy days filled with late nights laughing so hard my stomach cramps, walks at the park cozied up in his green sweater, and kisses that literally make me weak in the knees on my porch.

I haven't invited him into my apartment yet. One, because Jenny's usually there and somehow manages to walk by the window every time Wyatt's face is anywhere near mine and makes cat-calling noises. But mostly it's because I'm afraid if I invite him in, I won't let him leave. And I'm not ready for any...overnight guests. I've never had an overnight guest. I never got that far with the infamous Matty

Chase and I was so focused on school in college, nothing ever got far enough for there to be an overnight guest.

But if there's anyone I'd invite to stay, I know it would be Wyatt. But there's no hurry. We have all the time in the world. And I plan on cherishing every single second of that time.

Maybe it's the time of year, Christmas lights everywhere and snow covering every inch of the ground, but something about life feels more magical lately.

And I don't think it has anything to do with the holidays.

"So, mom says you have a boyfriend," Logan interrupts my thoughts from across the dining room table on Monday night.

"What?" I ask in a hushed tone. I don't know where she is, but I'm not ready for her to hear this conversation just yet.

"I'll take that as a yes."

"How does she even know?"

"You didn't tell her?"

"No, I was trying to keep that information to myself for a bit."

"How long have you been seeing him?"

"We just started dating a couple weeks ago."

"Oh, she made it sound like you guys have known each other for a while."

I shrug. "I mean, we've known each other for, like, three months."

"Where did you meet him?" Anna, Logan's wife, chimes in, taking the chair next to me.

"At work," I mumble.

"I'm sorry, little miss Perfect Lucy Rae is dating a *client*?" Landon drops his hand on his chest in mock surprise. He gives me a not-so-sly wink, like the fact that I'm dating someone from work is totally new information to him.

"Leave her alone!" his wife, Samantha, slaps him on his arm. "Tell us about him."

"Well, his name is Wyatt and he's..." I trail off. Where do I even start? He's beautiful, he's kind and understanding. He listens, he's funny.

"Aw," Samantha croons. "Someone's in love. Just look at the blush on her face."

"When do we get to meet this guy?" Logan asks.

I glare at him. "Not for twelve years. And that's if you're lucky."

Samantha and Anna laugh as Landon narrows his eyes. "Maybe you should invite him to Monday night dinner next week."

"Who are we inviting to dinner next week?" my mom asks suddenly appearing out of nowhere.

"No one," I practically yell and her eyes widen. "I just mean, who would we invite? It's family only. And the week before Christmas. I'm sure he has plans."

"Well, I mean, I think mom would make an exception for someone like this," Logan says with a smirk. I throw my wadded napkin at his head. "It never hurts to ask."

"Children, behave," my mom chastises as she sits next to Landon. "Who are we talking about?"

I shoot a glare at Logan before I answer. "Just a friend of mine, Mom. No big deal."

"Well, who is the friend? They're more than welcome to come."

"His name is Wyatt."

"Oh!" she practically glows. "Is this your new boyfriend?"

"He's not my boyfriend," I argue. I mean, we've been out almost every day for the last two weeks, but we haven't exactly had the defining the relationship conversation yet.

"Well, you'll have to invite him. I'd love to meet him!" My mom says with a huge grin.

"I'll let him know," I mumble as I shoot daggers at my brothers who are both trying to hide their smiles.

"Lucy," I hear as I'm about to chuck a roll at my brother's head. I unclench my fist, the roll dropping to the floor as I turn to see my dad in the doorway. "You want to come in my office for a minute? I want to talk to you."

His voice is serious, his gaze even more so and my stomach starts to flip as I reply, "Sure."

I walk slowly behind him as we make our way down the hall and into Luke's old room that was renovated into an office after he got married twelve years ago.

My dad sits in his chair behind his desk and I tentatively take a seat across from him.

"We got the final check for the Reed project," he starts.

So we're having this conversation now, I guess.

It's been on my mind nonstop the last two weeks, Wyatt's words tattooed in my brain.

You're your own person. You're incredible because of what you have accomplished.

He understood my fear so well, nailing it right on the head. It's the biggest reason I've avoided this conversation for the last year. Why I've busted my butt to do far more than was expected of me to prove myself to everyone. When I was really just trying to prove to myself that I was good enough.

"Yeah, everything went great."

"So I heard. Mr. Reed left you quite the review." He turns the computer screen to me and I begin to read the website review that has Wyatt's name at the bottom of it.

Snow Better Builders is beyond exceptional. Communication throughout the entire project could not have been better. The crew was professional and respectful. Miss Snow exceeded all expectations by providing constant updates throughout the twelve weeks and stepping up and supporting her team with not only words but actions.

Miss Snow is not afraid of hard work or difficult conversations, and she misses absolutely nothing. Her attention to detail is extraordinary, and she is the main reason I'm choosing to give my first ever written review to Snow Better Builders.

I have to fight back tears as I read the review not once, but twice. He told me a couple days ago he was going to leave a review on our website. I told him he had to be honest, and he simply kissed me in response. I didn't care much what the review said after that.

"Wow," is all I manage in my dad's office.

"Yes, very good review."

He leans back in his chair, adjusting the collar of his grey button up. "I'm proud of you Lucy Rae. Mr. Reed wasn't the only one to sing your praises. Jared's been telling me how wonderful you've been doing for months."

"Really?"

He smiles. "You're good, Lucy. You're really good."

I blush lightly as I smile in return. "So, what, uh, exactly does that mean?"

He stares at me for a long moment, scrutinizing what I'm not sure. Finally, he rests his elbows on the desk and asks, "Are you sure this is what you want?"

"Dad, I can do this," I start, but he holds a hand up to stop me.

"Lucy, I am very aware of your capabilities. I have no doubt that you could be the top project manager in the state if you put your mind to it."

The praise shocks me. I physically jerk back in surprise, my glasses sliding down my nose. I adjust them on my face and look at him. "I'm confused."

He just chuckles.

"If you think I'd be so good then how come you keep telling me it's not the right time whenever I bring it up?"

He sighs, leaning back in the chair again. "Because I want you to go be a big, bad architect and take the world by storm. I want you to do great things, Lucy."

I let his words sit for a moment, dissecting each one, trying to understand how we got here when it suddenly clicks what he means. "*Snow Better Builders* is big, Daddy."

He gives me a smile that says, *sure it is.* "I don't want you to feel pressured to join the family business or feel like you have no other options. You're an incredible architect, Lucy. You should be working for the biggest architecture firms in the city! Not planning thousand-square-foot renovations in a small town."

"Dad," I start, leaning across the desk. "I don't want to work at some big architecture firm in the city. I want to be here. I want to be close to family and work alongside you," I smile and he offers the faintest one back. "Actually, I uh, already had a little architect project."

His eyebrows raise. "Yeah?"

"Yeah, um, my sketch kind of got mixed up with the one's I commissioned for *Abe's Place* and well...they picked mine."

"You designed the expansion for the restaurant?" he asks, bewildered.

I simply nod.

A few different emotions cross his face in the span of four seconds, but the one that remains at the end is better than I could've hoped for.

His smile is wide, proud. "Lucy, it was beautiful. I saw all the pictures you loaded into the folder. I'm so proud of you."

"Really?" I whisper, tears forming in my eyes.

"Of course! You're extremely talented and I just don't want that talent to go to waste."

"Well," I wipe a tear from my cheek. "I'm really glad you said that because I was hoping I could start including my own designs as an option for the clients."

"I think that's a great idea," he says, squeezing my hand across the desk. "We can talk more about it in the office tomorrow. We should probably get back in there before your mother comes looking for us."

"Sounds good."

He stands from the desk and I follow suit. He wraps his arms around my shoulder as we head back into the dining room.

"Now, about that boy your mother was talking about."

I watch the snowflakes stick to the window until they melt as I wait for Wyatt's car to pull into my apartment parking lot. There's something about the snow that's very calming, but at this moment, nothing could possibly calm me down.

I've never brought a boy home to meet my family and I've been working out a way to ask Wyatt since I got home from dinner last night. My loving family that adores me and is great...but they're crazy.

I have three older brothers, for crying out loud! All of whom love to give me a hard time and believe there isn't a man in this universe who could possibly be good enough for me. Luckily, they trust me and know I can make good judgements, but there's a reason I've never brought anyone home. I need a ring on this finger before I subject someone to the chaos. Not that I'm saying Wyatt needs to propose today. Holy moly, I'm getting ahead of myself. It really is the stress, I swear.

I'd planned on asking him about meeting my family in passing while we were talking about something else, so I'd easily be able to change the subject if necessary. I didn't want to put any pressure on him to feel like he had to even if he didn't want to. Not that Wyatt is the kind of person who would do something he didn't want to. I'm pretty sure he would be honest and tell me it was too soon.

But I'm in uncharted territory.

I hear his feet walk up the steps and I take a deep breath to calm myself, but it doesn't help. The second the door opens it all stammers out of me in a fast, slurred together sentence.

"WillyoumeetmyfamilyonMonday?"

His eyes widen to saucers. "I'm sorry, what?"

I'm so flustered I don't even have time to appreciate Wyatt in a baseball hat and sweatshirt.

"My family. Would you like to meet them?"

"Oh," he chuckles. "Sure. When?"

I release a huge sigh. "Next week. Our Monday night dinner. They want you to come next week."

He steps through the doorway and closes it behind him. He gives me a light peck on the cheek. "Sure, I can do that."

"Really? That's it?"

"What do you mean?"

"I don't know," I throw my hands up. "Isn't meeting the parents' kind of a big step?"

He shrugs. "I mean, I guess it can be, but it doesn't have to. Your family lives close, they invited me to dinner. Not a big deal."

"Are you sure?"

He chuckles. "Yes, Lucy. I'm sure."

"You don't think it's too soon?"

He shakes his head. "No. We don't have to follow stupid, arbitrary rules simply because we're in a relationship."

His choice of words makes me pause. "What exactly do you mean by 'relationship'?"

"I think you know what I mean," he murmurs, pulling me closer.

"I think so, too, but I really prefer verbal communication."

"But you're so good at reading people," he runs his lips from my ear down my neck.

"So, I can call you my boyfriend?"

"Only if I can call you my girlfriend."

"That's fair," I giggle as he nibbles on my ear. "That tickles."

"I know, that's why I do it," he grins. "I'll do anything to make you giggle like that."

He leans down, nibbling once again, drawing the same giggle out. He laughs bright as I pull myself from his grasp with a ridiculous grin on my face.

"Oh, I almost forgot!" I jump a little wondering how I could've even forgotten. Something about his kisses have that effect on me.

"What?"

"I talked to my dad."

"And?" he presses, squeezing my waist once.

"I am officially *Snow Better Builders* new project manager!"

His arms wrap around me instantly, lifting my feet off the floor. "I'm so proud of you. I told you it would all work out."

"I know! I don't even know what I was so worried about. I guess I just thought he didn't believe in me enough to give me the promotion, but we worked it all out and that's not the case at all! He even said I could start including my own designs in our portfolios."

"I'm so happy for you, Lucy." He kisses my cheek.

"Thanks! I'm happy for me too."

He kisses me once more before he asks, "You ready to go?"

"Yes, I just have to grab my shoes." I skip off to my room and slip on my shoes too quickly that I fumble over the laces. "So," I say as I make my way back to his side. "We just defined the relationship, huh? It was that simple?"

"Yeah," he smiles. "Should it have been more complicated?"

"I don't know. I've never really defined it in words before. One second you're making out in the back of a car and then next you're not. That's usually how boys want to define it."

"Good thing you found a man," he waggles his eyebrows.

I giggle and give him a playful shove. I open the coat closet to find a jacket. "Just promise me you won't immediately start calling me stupid pet names now that we're 'official'."

"What's wrong with pet names?"

"I just don't like them. I think they're cliché. Explain to me why people immediately start calling each other 'babe' once they're in a relationship. What's wrong with the names we've been called our whole lives that our parents put a lot of time and effort into choosing? I like my name. Particularly when you say it."

The corner of his mouth lifts a little. "Really?"

He tilts his head slightly, somehow looking at me through his eyelashes even though I'm a foot shorter than him. Oh goodness, what have I done?

"You look beautiful, Lucy."

The blush that burns my cheeks is hot and bright and he laughs confidently. He's been doing that a lot lately, laughing. When I first met him he kind of had that whole broody, mysterious vibe going for him. Over the last few weeks, I've seen him open up a little and smile, a lot. I wonder what changed.

"I'm sure I could find a pet name you like."

"Doubtful."

He takes a step closer. "Sweetie?"

"Am I seven?"

Another step. "Honey."

"We're not eighty."

He's right in front of me now, my back pressing against the closet door. "Darlin'."

I scoff. "I'm sorry, I didn't realize we moved to Alabama."

"Love?"

"Oh, you never mentioned you had British roots," I deadpan.

He takes the last step to close all distance and leans down, his lips brushing my ear when he says, "Hey, baby."

You know when you read romance novels and they describe the male character's tone of voice by saying he growled? I've always laughed at that. Jenny tells me I just don't understand and I need to read more. But really, what does it even mean? I don't think anyone really knows. People just write it because, for some reason, there's a collective agreement in the book world that it's sexy. But men don't actually growl.

Or so I thought.

There's a 98% chance Wyatt just growled in my ear. And I really, *really,* want him to do it again. Or maybe fifty times.

I have no response. I've been left speechless from the impossibly sexy bookish growl and I can feel the burn on my cheeks that he brushes with his finger as he kisses my neck and says, "Bingo."

He stands upright with the smuggest smile I've ever seen.

I shake my head. "Nope. Definitely not baby."

He laughs loudly as he takes my hand and pulls me outside.

chapter twenty-eight
wyatt

"Uncle Wyatt, Uncle Wyatt!"

The little voice shrills immediately as I open the front door. He bolts so fast into my arms I almost don't catch him.

I haven't stopped by in weeks, my days filled with the restaurant and any spare time filled with Lucy.

I got an earful from Walker a few nights ago at the restaurant that Ellie was so upset I'd gone weeks without even a text to tell her how things were going. When I got home last night, I had twelve unread messages from Ellie. Ten of them were in all caps. I finally called her and wished I didn't. Ellie can be mean when she feels left out. I decided this morning I'd stop by since it was Sunday and the restaurant was closed. I needed to find out what the

Christmas dinner plans were anyway. Maybe I'd even mooch off a little dinner.

Some things never change.

"What's up, buddy?"

"I'm going to be a big brother!" he exclaims.

His words catch me off guard and I glance over at Ellie who has a tentative smile on her face, waiting for my reaction. Walker told me they weren't telling Lincoln until her third trimester. Though, one look at Ellie and her growing stomach tells me she's probably in her third trimester. I've been so caught up in Lucy I haven't even had time to think about the pregnancy.

The last few weeks have been the biggest reprieve from all the weight I've been carrying. Somehow with Lucy, nothing seems so bad. Even when she asks the hard questions, they're not so bad to answer. She brings comfort to every situation, every conversation and I've never felt so at peace in my life.

Until now.

Everything leaves my brain, my body goes rigid, and I feel like I'm in a trance. All thoughts of Lucy disappear and that full feeling in my chest is replaced by broken shards of glass, cutting my airways.

"That's awesome, buddy," I manage after what feels like an hour, but there's no levity in my tone. It's empty. All emotion gone.

"I hope it's a boy and then he can play soccer with me!"

"Yeah, that would be awesome." I force a smile and drop him on the floor.

"I'm gonna go through my toys and see what I can play with him." He runs down the hall and out of sight.

Ellie waddles into the entry way with me and I see just how much she's grown. How close we are to another little person running around. "You didn't tell us you were coming over."

I stick my hands in my pockets, standing awkwardly in the same spot, unable to move. My voice is quiet and stiff when I say, "I was just on my way home. Thought I'd stop by."

"Oh, well, your mom is in town and she's grabbing the stuff to make cupcakes with him later. I want to hear everything about your date. Or dates! I'm sure your mom does too," she smiles, but she's tentative. Still waiting for me to react.

"No worries. I'll just, uh, I'll just head home. I'll stop by another time."

"Wyatt..." she says with a tilt of her head and that same, sad look in her eyes that I used to see all the time. The worry, the pity, the fear. I don't want to see any of it.

I know she just cares about me and wants me to be happy, but it only offers a constant reminder of all the things I've ruined. All the things I've given up.

"Please, Ellie. Don't."

"Don't what?" she asks, moving closer, but I take a step back.

"Don't look at me like that."

"Like what?"

"Like you feel sorry for me."

She doesn't respond and we stand in the silence awkwardly before I turn on my heel without a word and walk through the front door.

It's all too much. The reminder of all that could've been, the reminder of what is. Lincoln's small voice, exclaiming his excitement for a little brother or sister. His simple understanding of his family. Wondering if he would be as excited to know the truth. If he would understand what a half-sibling was or if he would be angry knowing what I did. Or what I didn't do. The anger, the guilt, the sadness, the regret – it all knots in my stomach, twisting together making me feel like I'm going to throw up.

All I can think about is the drink I know would numb that knot.

I unlock my car and open the door when Ellie scurries out the front door. "Wyatt, please don't go."

I stand awkwardly behind the open door and look up at her, the sun glaring in my eyes. "Are you ever going tell him?"

"What?"

"Lincoln. Are you ever going to tell him the truth?"

She stares at me wide-eyed for a beat before she suddenly scowls.

"No," she retorts. "You chose this, Wyatt. I'm glad you got yourself together and that you're in his life. You have no idea how happy that makes me." She moves until she's right in front of me. "And I know this pregnancy has to be hard on you, I won't belittle that. I'm sure it's just dredging up the past and that hurts, but you don't get to turn around and try to erase that past. Walker is his dad. Not you." She takes another step closer until she can poke me in the chest. "Just like *you* wanted."

She's right, of course.

But that doesn't make it hurt any less.

"I'm sorry, Ellie," I say quietly, trying to fight off the tears I can feel forming. I don't remember the last time I cried.

She sighs and says more calmly, "No, Wyatt. Don't apologize. Lincoln is here because of you and he loves you so much. You're his Uncle Wyatt. You're, like, his favorite person."

I know it's meant to reassure me. To remind me how loved I am, but all it does is remind me that I'm Uncle Wyatt. That all I will ever be is Uncle Wyatt.

She waits for a response, but it doesn't come. I don't know what to say. I don't know how to fix all the things I've broken.

She wraps her arms around me suddenly, squeezing tight. "Please don't spiral," she whispers against my neck before pulling away.

It's scary how easily she can see the signs. It makes sense, though. She was with me through the worst of it. She knows better than anyone how quickly I can unravel.

"I'm fine, Ellie."

She gives me a look of disbelief. "Anytime I've ever said I was fine, I was lying."

chapter twenty-nine
lucy

"What do you think about going into the city for New Year's Eve?" I ask when he picks up the phone Sunday evening. "I know, I know, New York City is absolutely insane, but my uncle has a little condo and you can see the ball drop from there so we could avoid the crowds."

Wyatt and I have only been officially dating for almost a week, but it feels much longer than that. I've known him for three months and even that doesn't seem real.

I used to laugh at people like me. The ones who were talking about how their partner was the one after a month of dating. But I get it now. I know what it's like to find someone who instantly understands you. To find the person you want to share every single part of you with because you know they'll still want you, even after they've seen the ugly parts.

The person who's just there no matter what.

I don't think it takes years to know if the person you're with can be that for you. Either they are or they aren't. If you're waiting around for two years trying to determine if they're the best person for you, they probably aren't.

"With Christmas next weekend, we probably won't see much of each other," I go on. "I know you have some plans with your family. But I don't know, New Year's Eve could be fun."

I can hear the sound of the TV in the background and his voice is bland when he mumbles, "Yeah."

"Well, don't sound so excited. If you're sick of me already just say so." I laugh at my joke, but I hear nothing from the other end of the phone.

"Wyatt, are you still there?"

"Yeah."

"Are you okay? Or are my jokes just not that funny?" I chuckle. "If you'd rather spend New Year's Eve with your family, I totally get it."

"I'm fine," he replies dully, not even acknowledging the holiday.

All humor is gone and I'm actually getting worried. "Wyatt?"

He sighs loudly.

"What's wrong?"

The silence is deafening. I wait impatiently, chewing on the tip of my pen.

"I bought a six pack on my way home."

I'm not sure what's happened, or why he would buy the alcohol or even tell me. But I know how important his sobriety is to him. "I'll be there in ten."

I make it there in only five minutes and when he answers the door I have to do my best to hide my face. His hair is rumpled, and he has dark circles under his eyes. He's wearing sweatpants and a dingy t-shirt I think used to be white in another life.

"What happened?"

"You didn't have to come."

"Well, I did, so suck it up." I walk past him, not waiting for an invite, unsure if he'll even give me one. I glance around the apartment quickly, but find no trace of alcohol. That's a good sign.

"I threw it out."

I turn back to him and he's leaning against the closed front door. More like slumping against it.

"Good," I nod. "Why did you buy it?"

He stares at me for a long time. "You're too good for me, Lucy. Too good for any of this. You should just go."

"Don't pull that martyr crap with me, Wyatt. No one is perfect."

"I'm not like you. I've done bad things."

"Who hasn't?"

"You don't understand."

"Then explain it to me."

"I'm not a good person."

I want to argue the point, but I know he won't let me. Of course, he's a good person. I see it in the way he plays with his nephew and the way he talks about his family. I see it in the way he will nudge me to his right side when we're walking down the sidewalk so he's closest to the street. I see it in the way he asks about my day and genuinely wants the answer.

"No one is perfect," I say again.

He shakes his head. "You don't know the things I've done."

In the back of my mind, I want to ask what he's done. I can't imagine it's nearly as bad as he thinks. I know he used to drink a lot, but I know many people who used to drink a lot. My brother being one of them. Logan drank a lot in college, who didn't? I mean, I didn't, but most of my friends did.

But it also doesn't matter who he was. I know who Wyatt *is*.

"When I was in high school," I start, hoping to get through to him. "I lied to the principle and told her a girl had thrown bleach on my hair in the locker room after gym."

The surprise shows on his face, but barely. All of his emotions far, far away. "Why?"

"Because I'd found her kissing my boyfriend on the football field and I'd gotten a bad hair bleach the weekend before. I was seventeen."

"Did they believe you?"

I nod. "Yeah, she got suspended for a week. Senior year."

"Did you ever tell the principle the truth?"

"No, I didn't. Actually, you're the only person I've ever told. Even Jenny doesn't know."

He stares at me for a long time before he sighs. "It's not the same, Lucy."

"Why?"

"Because..." he runs a hand down his face.

I grab his face in my hands and force him to look at me. "Don't play games with me. If you're going to walk away, I deserve to know why."

He's speaking before I've even finished. "Lincoln is mine."

"What?"

"Lincoln is my biological son."

It takes a minute for the words to register. He looks at me with a pained expression. My hands fall from his face and I take a step back when I realize the look on his face is fear.

He's afraid this will be too much for me.

"How?" I ask in the calmest voice I can muster.

He raises a brow. "Ellie and I had..."

I shake my head, "I know that part! I'm just confused. I thought Dannie and Walker had been together for years."

"They got together when she was pregnant with Lincoln."

"Lincoln calls you Uncle Wyatt."

He nods. "He doesn't know. Walker's his dad. I'm not."

"But you are his dad," I argue, still wrapping my brain around it all.

"No, Lucy, I'm not. Walker's name is on the birth certificate."

"Why?"

He takes a deep breath before he says, "I signed away all my parental rights before he was born. I signed papers stating I was an unfit parent, and I didn't show up to any court dates."

He looks at me dead in the eye. "I gave him up before he was even born."

chapter thirty
wyatt

In her defense, she doesn't gasp or scowl or freak out. She doesn't do anything actually.

We stand in silence for the longest time and I'm waiting for the moment she decides this is all too much and she walks out the door or tells me I'm a horrible person and she can't be with someone so careless.

But she doesn't do any of those things.

"Why?" she whispers.

I didn't expect questions. I didn't except anything.

"I wasn't in a good place," I say, dropping onto my couch. "I was on some serious drugs back then. If I'm honest, I don't really remember the day I signed the papers. I was really hungover and on all kinds of things I'd rather not say. All I knew was I couldn't have a kid. I didn't even have my own apartment. I was crashing on a friends couch who ended up kicking me out that day. I stayed in a shelter for three days because I had nowhere to go."

Her voice is so soft when she says, "You stayed in a homeless shelter?"

I nod.

I can see tears forming in her eyes, but she blinks them away before they can fall as she takes the seat next to me on the couch. "What changed?"

I shrug. "Not much at first. I didn't really care the first little while. Then I got sober enough one day to realize what I'd done. That just led to some more drinking and even worse drugs."

"How long exactly have you been sober?"

"Almost five years."

"What happened five years ago?"

I remember the day I decided so vividly. My brain goes back in time as the words pour out of my mouth.

"It was November in the city. Lincoln was four or five months I guess. I hadn't seen Ellie since she told me about him and Walker even before then.

"I was walking home one morning from the bar, pounding headache. I'd had too much to drink and I was walking slow. It had just snowed the night before, the first of the season, and the park was packed full. Kids were yelling and laughing, chatter everywhere. Everyone was making snowmen and having snowball fights.

"It was so loud, there was noise all around me, but I heard a baby giggle. A bright, full baby giggle, and I turned my head in the direction it came from." I smile at the memory. His big pudgy cheeks, the biggest smile I'd ever seen. The laugh that broke my heart.

"I don't know what it was about that sound that had me turn my head. Instinct, I guess. I didn't even think about it. I heard his laugh and I just turned.

"I saw them making snow angels. Lincoln was just crawling through the snow and laughing so hard his face was bright red. He was bundled up in these big snow pants and a giant jacket. All I could see was his little face. Walker was throwing tiny snowballs at him and he just couldn't stop laughing. Ellie was laughing, too. Walker had the biggest smile on his face."

I wipe a tear that's fallen on my arm.

"They didn't see me. Even now, they don't know I saw them that day. I wanted to walk over and demand to see him, but I knew they wouldn't let me. Not until they were sure I was clean. So I got clean. I went to AA, I read all the books, started meditating. Once I was eight months sober, I asked if I could see him. It was just a couple days after his first birthday that I finally had the courage to show up at their restaurant. I didn't know exactly when his birthday was, but I figured it was June. The last time I saw Ellie was the end of May. I figured she'd had the baby not long after.

"Walker was livid. Yelled at me, told me to get the hell out and never come back. Ellie said much of the same. I went back every day for three weeks before she finally let me see him."

More tears fall down my cheek at the memory of holding my son for the first time. "That was the greatest day of my life."

Lucy takes my hand in both of hers and rubs her thumb over the back of my hand soothingly. "What was it, about that day, that made you change?"

"I saw my son for the first time." I wipe another tear from my face. "You know, you hear people talk about holding their babies for the first time and how they had no idea they could love something so much, but until you experience it for yourself you don't really understand it. I hadn't even held him, but I saw him. That was enough. My life changed that day. That was *my* son, life that I had created. He was a part of me," I choke up, barely getting the words out and Lucy squeezes my hand. "I realized in that moment that there were more important things in life than me. More important than my failures or insecurities. I didn't want to be my dad. He left because he cared about himself more than his family. Lincoln deserved better than that."

"He's really lucky to have you," Lucy whispers, wiping her own tears. "I know I didn't know you then, but I can tell how hard all of this has been on you. You're a good uncle, Wyatt. A good father."

I shake my head. "I'm not his father. My name isn't on the birth certificate."

"Maybe not in all aspects of the word, but one thing I know for sure is that my father would do anything for me. He'd give up everything if it meant I would find happiness in this world. You changed for Lincoln, but more importantly you gave him up. Whether you recognize it or not, you put Lincoln first. You knew he needed a better life than you could give him at the time. That's what fathers do. They put their kids first."

She pulls my hand to her mouth and drops a kiss. "A piece of paper doesn't change any of that."

Lucy stayed late. Around midnight, I promised her I was okay and she should get home. We were supposed to have dinner with her family the next night and I told her I'd pick her up at six.

"You don't have to meet my family right now, Wyatt. If you need some time or something, I can reschedule."

"I want to. I promise," I assured her with a slow kiss.

I slept like crap, my mind raveling on all the things Ellie has said over the years and more on what Lucy said.

That's what fathers do. They put their kids first.

I'd never thought of it that way before. I'm not so sure I believe that's what I did, but I'd like to think so.

I finally crawled out of bed around ten and decided I should stop by Ellie's. I feel bad for how I left things and she should know I'm okay.

I don't knock. I never knock.

"Anyone home?" I call, but only silence answers.

I walk through the small entryway and into the living room and still find no one. By now I should be able to hear Lincoln's loud screams or laughter or the pounding of his feet running around the house. I find his toys scattered about the floor, but I don't see or hear the kid anywhere.

I continue through the house, until I reach the kitchen and stop dead in my tracks when I hear voices on the other side of the wall in the master bedroom.

"No, Dannie," Walker says firmly.

"Walker, please, just hear me out – "

"No. He's *my* son. There's nothing to tell him."

"It's not that simple and you know it."

"We agreed, Dannie."

"I know we agreed, but – "

"He signed the damn papers!"

I startle back when I hear what I assume is Walker's fist slamming against the wall.

I try to ignore the pain in my chest at the vague memory of me signing those stupid papers. I did so much research after I came back to see what I could do to get out of it. There wasn't much. Dannie had a good lawyer and had everything in writing. All the drinking, the failed classes, the dropped scholarship, skipping football practice, my DUI - every single bit of my past was in writing, proving I wasn't a fit parent. And I sighned it. I admitted to doing all of those horrible things and that I was too dangerous to be around my own kid. Then I didn't show up to any of the court dates. I had a chance, and I blew it. I signed one little piece of paper that told the entire world I wasn't good enough and then didn't even go to court to speak on my behalf or Lincoln's. All parental rights lost, just like that. Honestly, I was lucky they even let me come back. Luckier still that Walker let me work for him. I wouldn't have made it without him. Without either of them.

And I hate how much I still feel like I owe them.

How much I owe Lincoln that I'll never be able to make up.

"That was years ago, before Wyatt got clean. Things are different, Walker."

I'm surprised to hear her fighting for me. Especially after she told me quite the opposite just yesterday.

"No."

"Where are you going?" I hear Ellie's voice, followed quickly by Walker's footsteps as he comes around the corner.

He stops when he sees me, Ellie right behind him.

"What are you doing here?" he barks.

I clear my throat awkwardly. "I came to see Lincoln."

"Mom took him to the park," he snaps, grabbing his coat off the rack in the entry.

"Walker, where are you going?" Ellie asks.

"Out," is all he says before slamming the front door behind him.

She turns to me then. "How long have you been here?"

I shift on my feet uncomfortably. "Long enough."

"I'm sorry, Wyatt. You shouldn't have had to hear that."

"It's fine. It's my fault anyway."

"It's not your fault."

I scoff half-heartedly. "Everything's my fault."

She gives me a look of pity that has me taking a step back, toward the front door. "You guys don't need to be fighting because of me. I don't expect anything, Ellie. I shouldn't have even brought it up. It was just a rough day. Walker's right."

"Wyatt..." she trails off.

"I should go," I brush a kiss to her forehead as I walk past her.

"Are you sure you're okay?" she asks in that tone I've heard too many times before. The same tone I heard every time I came to her dorm room high as a kite and she asked me if I was okay. Or when she'd asked if I'd made it to my classes that day or if I was coming to her piano concerts. All the times she asked me how many drinks I'd had the night before.

A tone that tells me just how broken she thinks I am.

I swallow the lump in my throat. "I'm fine, Ellie. I promise. Tell Lincoln I'll come by tomorrow."

"Okay," she whispers, and I walk out the door. The only thought in my head being where the closest liquor store is.

chapter thirty-one
lucy

I've text him twice and he hasn't responded.

Ten minutes late isn't horrible, but he's never late. He's annoyingly punctual, in fact.

I wouldn't be that worried, if I'd heard from him at all in the last twenty-four hours, but he didn't respond to my texts this morning that I sent to make sure he was okay.

I send a quick text to my family to let them know we're running a little late.

I try calling him again and there's still no response.

My mom text me early this morning to confirm that we were still coming and I replied yes, because Wyatt had said just last night that he still wanted to go.

My mom texts me again after I tell them we'll be late, but I refuse to respond to any of their messages until I get answers. Especially the ones from my brothers.

Luke: Mom wanted to know if she should bring out the home movies. I told her absolutely. You're welcome.

Landon: Luke brought out the home movies. I tried to snatch the one of you potty training, but he beat me to it. Just know I was on your side.

Eventually, I put my phone face down on the kitchen table and pace the living room.

I run through every possible scenario in my mind as to the reason he is now twenty-two minutes late.

He got in a car accident on the way over here.

He lost his phone and is, in fact, running late because he was trying to find it.

He decided I'm not worth it and he's avoiding me instead of breaking up with me to my face.

My phone suddenly starts vibrating and I snatch it so fast, it slips right through my fingers.

"Dagnabbit," I mumble as I snatch it off the floor.

Still not Wyatt. It's an unknown number that I ignore with a loud groan. The spam calls these days are out of control, but when they call again and then again, I pick it up simply out of curiosity.

"Hello?"

"Is this Lucy?" A woman asks.

I sound a little too aggravated when I ask, "Who's asking?"

"This is Dannie Reed. Wyatt's sister-in-law."

My heart immediately starts to race. Something has to be wrong if she's calling. "Is he okay?"

"Sorry to bother you, I got your number from their business file, I hope that's alright."

"Of course. What's going on?"

"Well, Wyatt left here this morning a little...upset. I haven't been able to get ahold of him and I'm probably being dramatic, but I'm a little worried. Have you talked to him?"

"No, I haven't. He was supposed to pick me up a half hour ago to meet my family for dinner. He isn't answering my calls either."

She swears under her breath.

"I'll stop by his apartment," I tell her, already grabbing my shoes.

"Are you sure?"

"Yeah, let me see if I can find him."

"Thanks, Lucy. I'm glad he has you."

I hang up the phone with the promise that I will let her know if I find him. I grab my keys off their hook and hope he's home. And that he's just as glad that he has me.

wyatt

I wake up to someone banging on my head.

I have no idea how long I was asleep. Hours, days, who knows at this point. I lost track of time about the time I pulled out the second bottle.

It takes me a minute to realize there isn't anyone pounding on my head. It must just be the world's worst hangover, because it won't stop. I should get up and drink some water. Instead, I roll over with a rough groan and grab the bottle on the nightstand that's still half full.

I take a swig that burns going down, my throat dry from sleep.

The banging continues and it's not until I hear a voice on the other side that I realize it's someone knocking on the front door.

"Wyatt, open the darn door right now! I know you're in there, I saw your car in the parking lot."

Lucy.

Her name swirls in my head, intertwined with the pain and the alcohol. The one bright light in the midst of all the darkness.

"Go away," I say loud enough for her to hear.

"Seriously?" she shouts back. "My entire family is asking me why you blew them off. I'm not going anywhere. Open the freaking door, Wyatt!"

Even in the hangover haze, I know she means business when she says 'freaking'. I stumble to the front door and simply unlock it.

It takes her approximately two seconds to burst through the door.

"Are you kidding me?" she says from the doorway.

I ignore the question and sit on the dining room chair, grabbing whatever bottle I left on the table last night.

"I swear – " she begins, but her attitude immediately fades as she take me in. I do my best to focus on her through the fog, but it would be easier if she would stop swaying.

She's wearing leggings with an oversized green sweater. Her hair is in two tiny ponytails and her lips are just lightly pink, most likely from the cold. It takes me a minute to realize she's wearing my green sweater. The one I gave her the other day when she was cold. She never did give it back.

She looks so beautiful.

And she shouldn't be here.

"Go away," I say again.

"Wyatt, what's wrong?" she asks much quieter this time. Her eyes take in my apartment. The mess of clothes strewn about and a half-eaten plate of food on the kitchen counter. She stops on every empty bottle she finds, I'm sure counting them. There can't be that many, but I lost count around bottle four. And that was just the beer.

Her eyes finally land on me and I avoid making eye contact, not wanting to see the look of disappointment I know I'll find if I do. I stare at her lips when I mumble, "Just get out." I take a swig of I don't know what at this point. I bought more than a six pack. I remember the guy at the checkout counter, eyeing me. It wasn't until I got through the beer that I opened the whiskey. That's what finally made me throw up before I crawled into bed. I used to hold my liquor much better than this.

"Wyatt, please," she takes a step closer, but I stand suddenly, swaying on my feet.

"Get out!" I scream, my voice going hoarse. "I don't want you here, Lucy!"

I throw the half empty bottle of alcohol at the wall by her head. Glass shatters across the floor and liquid slides down the wall, spraying everything around it, including her. To her credit, though, she doesn't move. She doesn't even flinch. "Go away!"

She plants her feet, sticks her chin up and says in a forceful voice, "No."

I just stare at her.

She doesn't move. Her eyes glare into mine and she crosses her arms across her chest.

"I'm not leaving, Wyatt. So, you can scream and yell and throw whatever the heck you want at me, but I'm not leaving."

I'm not quite sure what to say. What to do.

Everyone leaves. My drinking buddies in college would always drop me at my dorm room when I got so bad, I couldn't walk on my own. My sister wouldn't even let me into her house. My mom had to call the cops on me to have me arrested for trespassing when I showed up to her house wasted as can be. Even Ellie walked away, slamming the door in my face without so much as a backwards glance.

But Lucy stays put.

"Why?" I ask so quietly, I don't know how she hears me.

Her gaze softens and she takes slow, tentative steps until she's right in front of me. She takes my face in her hands carefully and brings my forehead to hers.

"Because I love you."

Three words, eight letters and my whole world crumbles.

I drop to my knees, sobbing from deep in my chest. My arms wrap around her waist so tight, in the back of my mind I worry I'll break her. She doesn't say any more. She simply runs her hands through my hair and lets me cry into her stomach.

Eventually she drops to my level and I pull her onto my lap, her legs straddling mine. She holds me just as tightly and I grip the back of her shirt.

"Don't leave me," I beg through the sobs.

She kisses the side of my head, and her arms tighten around me.

"I'm not going anywhere."

chapter thirty-two
lucy

He's still asleep.

I was able to get him into bed after he cried on the floor so long my legs started cramping from sitting on his lap. I pulled him onto the bed where he let me slip off his shoes and shirt that was so drenched in alcohol I threw it in the wash immediately. I covered him with the comforter, and he grabbed my hand tightly as he whispered, "Don't leave."

So, I stayed. I rummaged through his drawers until I found a shirt large enough to cover me and changed in his bathroom where I brushed my teeth with my finger and combed my hair with his one single hair brush that had the roughest bristles on planet earth. Something that made his perfectly flowy, only brushed when wet hair even more irritating. I made a mental note to buy him a new hairbrush.

By the time I made it out of the bathroom he was snoring slightly, laying on his side, so I took my time cleaning the mess of the apartment. There was a lot of alcohol, considering it had only been a day. A couple beer bottles were still half full, but it was the completely empty whiskey bottle that had my chest feeling tight. I threw everything in a giant trash bag I found under the sink and dropped it all in the trash outside.

Once the apartment was clean, and I sent a quick text to Dannie to let her know he was home and mostly okay, I carefully crawled into bed and wrapped my arm around his waist. I fell asleep with my cheek against his back listening to the sounds of his breaths.

I woke up about an hour ago. Sometime in the night we switched places. I can feel his breath on my neck and his arm is wrapped tightly around me, his legs intertwined with mine.

A million times I've considered leaving. I'd be lying if I said it was easy to stay last night. I was terrified what I would find when I walked through the front door. I expected alcohol, I expected anger. Heck, I expected drugs.

Nothing prepared me for what I'd actually find.

He was sitting in that chair looking so alone and afraid. So broken.

It broke my heart.

I couldn't leave him like that.

I knew he wouldn't hurt me. I'm not afraid of Wyatt. Even in his drunken stupor he would never hurt me.

I feel him shift behind me and his lips tickle my neck.

"You're still here." His voice is rough from sleep.

"I told you I wasn't leaving."

He kisses my neck. "What time is it?"

"Around eight, I think."

"Are you okay?"

A breathless scoff escapes. "I think I should be asking you that question. Not the other way around."

"Lucy," he whispers my name like a prayer and leaves a faint trail of kisses down my neck that causes goosebumps to rise on my arms.

"So, are you? Okay, I mean?"

"My head is killing me."

"There's some ibuprofen on your nightstand and a bottle of water."

"You're incredible."

He rolls over just long enough to swallow the pills, then he's back behind me, holding tightly.

"Can you tell me what happened yesterday?"

He sighs loudly and rolls away from me onto his back. I'm not taking that for a second. I turn over and rest my arm on his chest.

"Look at me, Wyatt. Tell me what's going on."

"I just...got into it with Ellie on Saturday and now Walker's pissed at me." He runs a hand down his face, exhausted. "I'm just sick of ruining everything."

I kiss his cheek. "You're not ruining anything. This is a difficult situation, Wyatt, for everyone. Lincoln is here because of you, that's something to be proud of. *He's* something to be proud of. What did Dannie say?"

He smiles faintly. "Exactly what you just said."

I can't help but smirk. "So, she's pretty smart?"

"Yeah."

"Can I ask you something?"

He nods.

"Do you think you made the right choice?"

He thinks for a moment. "Yes and no. It should be my name on the birth certificate. I feel like I denied my son before he was ever born. That's not fair to him or me. Obviously, I can't change that, but I don't regret what followed. I'm happy for Walker and Dannie, I think Lincoln is better off living with them than he would be living with me or any kind of shared custody agreement. I'm okay with the way things are right now, but..." he trails off unsure how to finish. I take his hand in my and rub it gently with my palm, giving him the time he needs. "I don't want him to think that I was ever ashamed of him or that I regretted any of it. Whether good or bad, I did what I thought was best at the time."

"He's going to know that. Lincoln loves you so much, that's never going to change. And someday, if or when he learns the truth, he'll understand because you raised him right."

He looks at me, eyes glistening with tears. "You don't think I'm a bad person?"

"You're the best person I know, Wyatt." I lean down for another kiss. "You may not see it, but what you did was extremely selfless. You did what you knew was right for your son. You gave him up. You and I both know that was the best decision for him."

"You're too good for me," he whispers.

I slap him playfully. "I'm gonna need you to stop saying that. I'm not interested in any of this martyr crap. You deserve to be happy."

He pulls me down and rolls over until he's leaning over me again. "I'm so sorry, Lucy."

"For what?"

"Everything. I'm sorry I yelled at you, I'm sorry I ignored you. I'm sorry I – " he stops abruptly and a look of horror crossing his face.

"What?" I ask.

"I threw a bottle at you," he whispers with so much fear and shame in his eyes. "Are you okay?" His fingers brush my cheeks and I think he might start crying again.

"You just threw a bottle at the wall, you weren't aiming for me."

"I shouldn't have thrown anything, not with you in the room."

I run my fingers down his cheek. "You didn't hurt me, I'm fine. But I can't do another night like this again."

He shakes his head. "There won't be another night like this, I promise. I swear."

He stares at me for the longest time, his thumb brushing my bottom lip. "Did you mean it?"

"Did I mean what?"

He swallows hard. "That you love me."

I shift more so I'm completely on my back, looking up at him leaning over me, and take his face in my hands.

"I love you, Wyatt."

His lips are on mine before I can even finish.

Wyatt has been extremely careful with me in the short time we've been together. We've kissed multiple times and it's incredible each time, but there was always this sense that he was holding something back. Now I realize he was trying not to get too close. Testing the waters before diving in. Making sure I felt what he felt before he committed. I know what it's like to worry that you're not good enough and I would never want Wyatt to feel that way. So I tighten my hands in his hair.

A low groan escapes from deep in his throat and he opens my mouth with his.

This kiss is so much more than any of the others. This kiss is all those suppressed feelings crashing against the wall like the beer bottle last night.

Is it possible to love someone this much so quickly?

His mouth is rough, his hands gripping my waist tightly. His body falls on top of mine and he shifts until I'm on top of him.

Yes. Yes it is.

He nips at my bottom lip before moving down my neck and brushing his tongue over my collarbone.

"Wyatt," I say breathlessly, when his hands stray to the hem of his shirt that's ridden up on my legs.

"I'm sorry," he says, his hands instantly moving higher on my back. "I got a little carried away. My morning alcohol breath probably isn't anything to write home about either."

I chuckle. "No, it's okay. I liked it."

He smiles my favorite crooked smile. "The morning alcohol breath? Noted."

I roll my eyes. "No, gross. Your teeth should be brushed. But I'm not mad about the little bit carried away part. Even with the morning breath."

He chuckles. "Me either."

His finger traces my face, running over my eyebrows, down my nose over my top lip, down my jaw, my neck, before tucking under the neck of his shirt. The warmth of his fingers leaving a trail down my skin, making me shiver. "This is my shirt."

"I needed something to sleep in."

"It looks good on you."

"It looks *better* on me, I think I might just keep it." I joke, but he suddenly turns serious. "What?"

"Thank you, Lucy."

"For what?"

"For staying."

"You don't need to thank me. I wouldn't want to be anywhere else."

"I do, though. I'm not always good at expressing my feelings, but I want you to know I'm grateful for you."

I smile warmly and kiss his cheek. "I'm grateful for you too, Wyatt."

He sits up suddenly, wrapping me in a hug. "There's something I need to do. I won't be gone long, will you still be here when I get back?"

"I told you," I grab his face and pull him in for a lingering kiss. "I'm not going anywhere."

chapter thirty-three
wyatt

I have stood on this doorstep more times than I can count. I've walked through the door without knocking. I spend more time here than I do my own home, but something about today feels different.

I take a deep breath and knock on the door.

It only takes a minute for it swing open to Ellie on the other side.

"Wyatt? What are you doing here? And since when do you knock?"

I stuff my hands in my pocket for something to do with them. "I just...didn't want to barge in."

She cocks her head to the side. "I'm glad you're okay. I was a little worried when we didn't hear from you."

"Yeah, sorry about that."

"I'm just glad you're okay."

"Me too," I smile.

"Look, Wyatt, about yesterday – "

"No, Ellie." She shouldn't be the one apologizing here. "Please, don't."

"Wyatt – " she tries again, but I stop her.

"I never apologized to you."

"What?"

"When I came back, I never said I was sorry. I never apologized for all the crap I put you through."

"You don't have to – "

"Let me finish, please."

Keeping quiet is not one of Ellie's strong suits, but she closes her mouth and waits.

"I was so angry at you for a long time, Ellie. I blamed you for most of my problems. You were the one person that was supposed to love me no matter what and you walked out on me."

I can see the tears pooling in her eyes and it makes my chest ache.

"But that wasn't fair. I made my own choices and the fact that you stayed as long as you did just proves how incredible you are. But I never said I was sorry. And I never thanked you for letting me back into Lincoln's life."

"I did love you, Wyatt. Leaving you wasn't easy." She wipes a tear from her cheek. "If it wasn't for Walker, I don't even know where I'd be."

She looks at me with those big eyes that always sucked me in. Looking at them now, I see the mother of my child, my brother's wife, his best friend.

My romantic feelings for Ellie have been gone for a long time, but I've spent too much time longing for what could've been.

But what's wrong with what is?

I have my family. I have my son. I have Lucy.

I have everything.

"Thank you, Ellie."

She steps onto the porch and wraps her arms around me, burying her face in my neck. "I was so worried about you. Don't ever ignore me after you walk out like that!"

I rub her back soothingly. "It was...a rough day, but I'm okay. I promise."

She pulls back just enough to look me in the eyes. "You smell like alcohol."

"Yeah, I forgot to brush my teeth before I left, sorry."

There's an edge in her voice when she says, "So, you were drinking."

I nod. "I was, but I'm not now and I know I shouldn't have been. No more alcohol."

"I won't tolerate alcohol, Wyatt."

"I know. Is Lincoln home?"

She shakes her head. "He had soccer practice this morning."

"Good, I don't want him to see me like this."

"Then don't be like this."

"I know, I'm sorry. I really am."

It's my turn to wipe a tear from my face. I've been crying so much the last few days, I don't even know what to do. I never used to cry. The first time in my life I ever cried was when I held Lincoln for the first time.

"I don't want to be like this, Ellie."

"Then don't be," she demands, her voice strong.

"I won't. Not anymore. I promise.

She watches me for a long time before she smiles. "Go get yourself put together. I expect to see you at Lincoln's game tonight."

"I'll be there."

"Sober?" she asks.

I nod. "Thank you, Ellie, really. For everything. And please tell Walker I'm sorry." I offer a smile before I turn toward my car.

"Wyatt?"

I look back to see her still in the doorway. "Lucy didn't think twice before going to your house. I called her and asked if she'd heard from you and she sprang into action, no questions asked. Don't shut her out. I spent a lot of years trying to fix everything myself and things would've been a lot better if I'd just let Walker help me. I guess I'm saying that you're not alone. It's okay to need someone. Lucy's great and she really cares about you. For all you know she just might be your saving grace."

I smile as Lucy's bright blue eyes and silly giggle pop into my head. "She's already saved me."

chapter thirty-four
lucy

I scoured his entire house. I did a load of laundry, ran the dishwasher. Did all the loud things I couldn't do while he was sleeping last night.

He told me he would be back and I promised him I would be here when he got back, but it's been four hours, and I haven't heard from him. I text him a half hour ago to see when he might be home, but no response.

By the second load of laundry, I'm anxious and wadding the clothes more than folding them.

Jenny text me multiple times last night after I told her not to wait up for me.

Jenny: I get a random text saying you won't be home for the night and then no response!

Jenny: I know you're with Wyatt Reed. I need details!

Jenny: You can't just go spend the night with a man and not tell me. I have best friend privileges you know.

The texts this morning have been even more colorful.

Jenny: I really hope you don't come home today and tell me you slept in separate beds. What a waste of a sleepover. But it would be so Lucy of you to do that.

Jenny: I got three different variations of popcorn and so many bags of sour candy I lost count. I'm ready to hear all the details!

Jenny: Love you!

I send her a quick text to let her know I was with Wyatt and I'm not sure when I'll be home. Before I can even put it down, it starts pinging with multiple message notifications. I chuckle under my breath and put her thread on silent.

I'd put my whole phone on silent, but I'm still waiting to hear from Wyatt.

I can't just be sitting in his house all day waiting for him to come back to me whenever he feels like it. That's not going to work for me.

Who does he think I am? Some little housewife ready to do his laundry, clean his house, make his meals and then just be waiting around? Nope. Not happening.

I grab my sweater, slip on my shoes, and throw my purse over my shoulder when the front door clicks.

Wyatt steps through the doorway in the same clothes he left in. I don't know why that surprises me. I have no idea what he was doing.

He has a bouquet of white flowers in one hand and a box of something tucked under his arm.

"Were you leaving?" He takes in my appearance with my jacket on and purse slung over my shoulder.

"Well, yes, Wyatt. I've been here for four hours. I wasn't going to wait all day. You didn't answer me when I called."

"I know, I'm sorry. I was kind of running all over the place."

He closes the door behind him and drops the flowers and box on the entry table.

"Care to share where "all over the place" is?"

He chuckles and my irritations becomes even more sour.

"This isn't funny, Wyatt. I'm not the kind of girl that just sits around waiting for you and then everything's fine because you brought me flowers and...and, is that chocolate?" I ask, eyeing the box on the table that has a very familiar logo on it. "That's from the chocolate shop on Main."

"It is."

I put my hands on my hips and do my best to pretend I have zero interest in the contents of that box. "And why might you have that?"

"Why? Do you want it?" He takes a step closer.

"I didn't say that."

His arms find my waist and he pulls me to him. "They're for you."

I shove his chest, but he's too strong and I stay put. "You can't just show up after disappearing for hours with flowers and chocolate and think that makes everything okay."

The smirk leaves his face and he sighs. "I know. I'm really sorry. I stopped by the talk to Ellie and then I went by the park to find Walker and we talked for a little bit."

"Are you guys okay?"

He nods once. "Yeah. It wasn't a very pleasant conversation, but in the end, I think we got it all worked out."

"Well, I'm happy for you. Family is important," I look at his chest beneath my hands.

His fingers brush my chin and he tilts my face up to look at him. "You're important, too, Lucy.

"Then why didn't you answer when I called?"

"My battery died. I didn't charge it last night. I really am sorry. I promise I won't do that again."

"And the drinking?"

He closes his eyes and his forehead falls against mine. "I don't think I can say sorry enough. I shouldn't have done any of the things I did last night and I can promise you it won't happen again."

"I want to stand by you, Wyatt. I want to support you. I'm not the kind of person who just walks out when things get hard, but this can't become a regular thing. I don't think I can do another night like last night."

"You should'nt have had to do it last night."

I grab his face in my hands and force him to look at me. "I'm here for you, Wyatt. I will help you when you need help. I just need you to help me help you."

His eyes light up just a little. "So, you're staying?"

"If you'll still have me."

"I brought you flowers and chocolate."

"Yes, we covered that."

"No, Lucy, I've never bought anyone flowers or chocolate." He wraps his arms tighter around my waist. "You have no idea what last night meant to me. I've had support in my life, but never like that. People tend to walk out when they see the things you saw. But you..." he seems at a loss for words and I'm pretty sure I see tears forming in his eyes. Those tears are confirmed when his voice cracks on the word, "stayed."

"I never could've left you like that," I whisper.

"I know you won't like it when I say this, but I'm going to say it anyway. Don't interrupt."

I chuckle breathlessly. "I'll do my best."

"I don't deserve you."

"Wyatt," I start, but the look in his eyes has me closing my mouth tightly.

"Thank you," he chuckles. "I don't deserve you, but I promise you that I will do everything I can to become the man you deserve. One who you can rely on and stands by your side like you stood by mine."

"I love you, Wyatt."

"I love you, Lucy Snow."

His lips are on mine before my name has fully formed. He's soft and patient and his lips just barely part with a sigh when I feel a tear fall from his cheek to mine.

"Do I get to eat the chocolate now?" I ask as I pull away, wiping his face and mine.

He laughs his full, deep laugh and I can't help but kiss him again.

"Can I say something now?" I ask as he opened the chocolate.

"Of course."

"I know you think you don't deserve me and you know that I'm going to say that's a load of poo. But I need you too, Wyatt. I need your steadiness and your honesty. I need your humor and your listening ears. I need you, too."

He drops the chocolate box on the table and pulls me into him once again. His voice rumbles against my neck as he says, "I really don't deserve you."

I giggle as his breath tickles my neck. "How about we both agree right here and now that we both deserve each other?"

"Deal." He chuckles, kissing my neck one last time. "Now let's have some chocolate."

I smile as he opens the box and I catch a glimpse out the window. "It's snowing."

He kisses my cheek. "How about I make some hot chocolate and then we take a walk through the snow?"

I grab the box of chocolate and kiss his lips. "Sounds perfect."

epilogue
wyatt

"I can't believe you're getting married! You're only twenty-two. I mean, when I was your age," I start, but Ellie's glare has me backpedaling. "Uh, well, it doesn't matter what I was doing when I was your age."

"You look so handsome, sweetie," Ellie says with tear filled eyes as she straightens his pocket square.

"Great, you got Ellie crying. That's a feat man, she's never gonna stop now."

"Shut up," she swats my arm and wipes the tears away.

"Mom," Lincoln says. "Can I talk to Wyatt for a minute?"

"Of course. I should find my seat." She kisses his cheek. "Oh, one more hug, I can't believe you're getting married!" She hugs him so tight, I think he turns a little purple.

"Uh, Ellie, he has to be able to breathe in order to actually get married."

"Right, I'm sorry. I love you so much," she pats his cheek and offers me a smile before she leaves us alone.

"Are you okay?" I ask when the door closes behind her.

"Yeah, I just, uh..." he trails off, awkwardly messing with his lapels.

"Lincoln, you're supposed to be getting married in..." I glance at my watch. "Now. Whatever this is, I'm sure it can wait."

"No, Wyatt, I..." he looks me dead in the eye. "Dad told me."

"Told you what?"

"I know, Wyatt. He told me everything."

He gives me a meaningful look, trying to convey words he can't seem to get out. We stare at each other for a beat before it suddenly clicks.

I'm stunned. We all agreed we'd take the information to our grave. What was Walker thinking? Did Ellie know? Was it her idea?

"Honestly," he laughs under his breath, "he told me more than I ever wanted to know about you and mom."

"Are you...okay?" I ask tentatively.

He nods slowly. "I think so. I was really mad at first."

"Does your mom know he told you?"

He nods. "But he told me a lot about you. And the reasons why."

"Lincoln..."

"You don't have to say anything. I guess I just wanted to say thank you."

That catches me completely off guard. "For what? Abandoning you before you were even born? Did he tell you everything? That I never showed up to court? That I signed documents relinquishing all parental rights and stating I was an alcoholic who was too dangerous to be around?"

"Yes," he says confidently.

I look at him incredulously.

"Wyatt, I have an amazing family. I hit the jackpot with my parents. And I hit the jackpot because you knew you weren't ready. I'm sure that wasn't easy for you, signing those papers. But you did it because you wanted what was best for me, even if you say you don't remember or you did it for selfish reasons. Whatever the reasons are, I'm glad things turned out the way they did. So, yes, I'm saying thank you."

"You really are so much like Walker."

He laughs once. "He thinks I'm exactly like Mom."

There is a light knock on the door before Walker's face pops in. "It's time, Lincoln."

He nods with a smile. "I better go. Emma will kill me if I'm late."

He turns back to me and suddenly embraces me. I've never been a hugger, not even with my family. I can probably count on one hand the number of times I've hugged Walker.

"Thanks, Wyatt. For everything." He releases me before I can respond and walks through the door, Walker patting him on the back as he goes. Walker and I stand there for a moment after he's gone.

Walker's barely aged over the years. Apart from a few wrinkles around his eyes and full head of soft silver hair, he looks almost exactly the same. My hair just started greying, much later than his started. He blames it on Ellie. Says she'd turn any man's hair grey.

"Thank you," I finally manage.

He stuffs one hand in his pocket. "He deserved to know."

"He's pretty amazing. I owe that to you."

"You helped." He pats my shoulder.

"Thank you, Walker. For all the things you've done for me. For Lincoln and Ellie, too. You changed my life, man."

He turns and looks through the small window by the door, where we can see Lincoln walking up the steps to the dais. "You changed my life, too." He smiles and I think there's a tear in his eyes. "Now, let's go watch our kid tie the knot."

Walker finds his seat next to Ellie who's doing everything she possibly can not to cry.

Lucy grabs my hand the second I sit down. "You okay?"

I kiss her forehead. "Never better."

I look passed her to the twins, who are both smiling and laughing at I'm not sure what, their eyes on Lincoln. It took a long time for Lucy to convince me to have kids. Considering the last time I did, I failed miserably at fatherhood. I was terrified, but on our second wedding anniversary she surprised me with the news. We hadn't been trying long.

Lincoln had been so excited when he found out he was getting more cousins. They were born just two weeks after his tenth birthday. He was the best cousin and the best big brother to Leightyn.

Watching him grow up, watching all of them grow up, was a blessing. Seeing the choices they make and the direction life is taking them.

Lincoln's been the biggest joy to watch. Maybe it's because he's older and he's making such important decisions at this stage in his life. We were all surprised when he told us he was going to Arizona State University. He got a full ride academic scholarship to NYU, but he chose ASU. He claimed it was because they had a better sports medicine program, but we all knew it was because of a green-eyed, curly haired blonde he'd had a crush on since the summer of his freshmen year when she stayed with Walker and Ellie for a summer music program in the city.

Their mothers were thrilled. Ellie spent weeks on the phone with her friend, Penny, talking about all the what-ifs. Those what-ifs became a reality quickly. The day Lincoln graduated, we had a party in the Wright's backyard and Lincoln proposed in front of both families.

The wedding march begins and we all stand to watch Emma walk down the aisle, led by her father, Charlie.

Ellie wipes more tears from her eyes as she, and everyone else, watches the beautiful bride glide down the aisle.

I glance back at Lincoln and he, too, has tears in his eyes.

I see so much of myself in him. My height, my dark hair, my love for sports and so much more.

I see just as much of Ellie in him. His attitude and determination. His big round eyes and eagerness to try literally anything.

Most importantly, I see Walker in him. I see the way he listens to everyone's needs and puts them first. I see the way he's patient with his sister and even more so with his soon-to-be-wife. I see how compassionate he is and how he would do anything for anyone.

Lucy squeezes my hand again as Emma joins Lincoln and they clasp hands.

Life is messy. Lord knows, I made a mess of a lot of things.

But I wouldn't change a single minute of it. Because all of those messy moments got me right here.

And where else would I want to be?

THE END

acknowledgements

It's a little unprecedented, but I'm going to thank myself first. This is what happens when you go after what you want. I wouldn't be here if it wasn't for my overinflated ego that tells me I can do whatever I want. And for that, I'm grateful.

To my best friend, the person I never want to be away from. Scott, you are the greatest part of my life and a huge inspiration for this story.

To my nieces and nephews – each of you inspire me every day with your flare for life and your excitement and passions.

My parents who go to every single event I put on and buy more books than they would ever have anything to do with. Your support is everything.

My sisters, my editors. I love that I have sisters who are willing to gush about my writing, but also aren't afraid to tell me what's wrong and where I'm lacking. I need the praise and the criticism.

To the readers. Thank you for picking up my book. Thanking you for giving it a chance. It's not perfect, but it's mine.

And lastly, to Wyatt. You deserved redemption, you deserved a happy ending. And I'm so glad I was the one lucky enough to give it to you.

about the author

Kennie Mae Evvie was born and raised in California and has a degree in music. She learned how to tell stories through music and quickly fell in love with the power of words. She currently resides in Arizona where she spends most of her time playing with her nieces and nephews, baking cakes, playing music, and dreaming of fictional men. Shh! Don't tell her husband.

KEEP IN TOUCH

@kenniemaewrites

https://kenniemaewrites.com

www.ingramcontent.com/pod-product-compliance
Lightning Source LLC
Chambersburg PA
CBHW021024310726
48969CB00006B/1537